The characters and events portrayed in this book are fictitious. Any similarity to real persons - living or dead - is coincidental and not intended by the author.

ISBN 978-1-3999-6248-3

Cover design by: Tony Burke/Ryan Hurley/David Burke
Library of Congress Control Number: 2018675309
Printed in the United States of America

It's taken me a long time to write this little book. Thanks to Anna, Elsie, Joe and my brother Dave for their help, support and understanding.

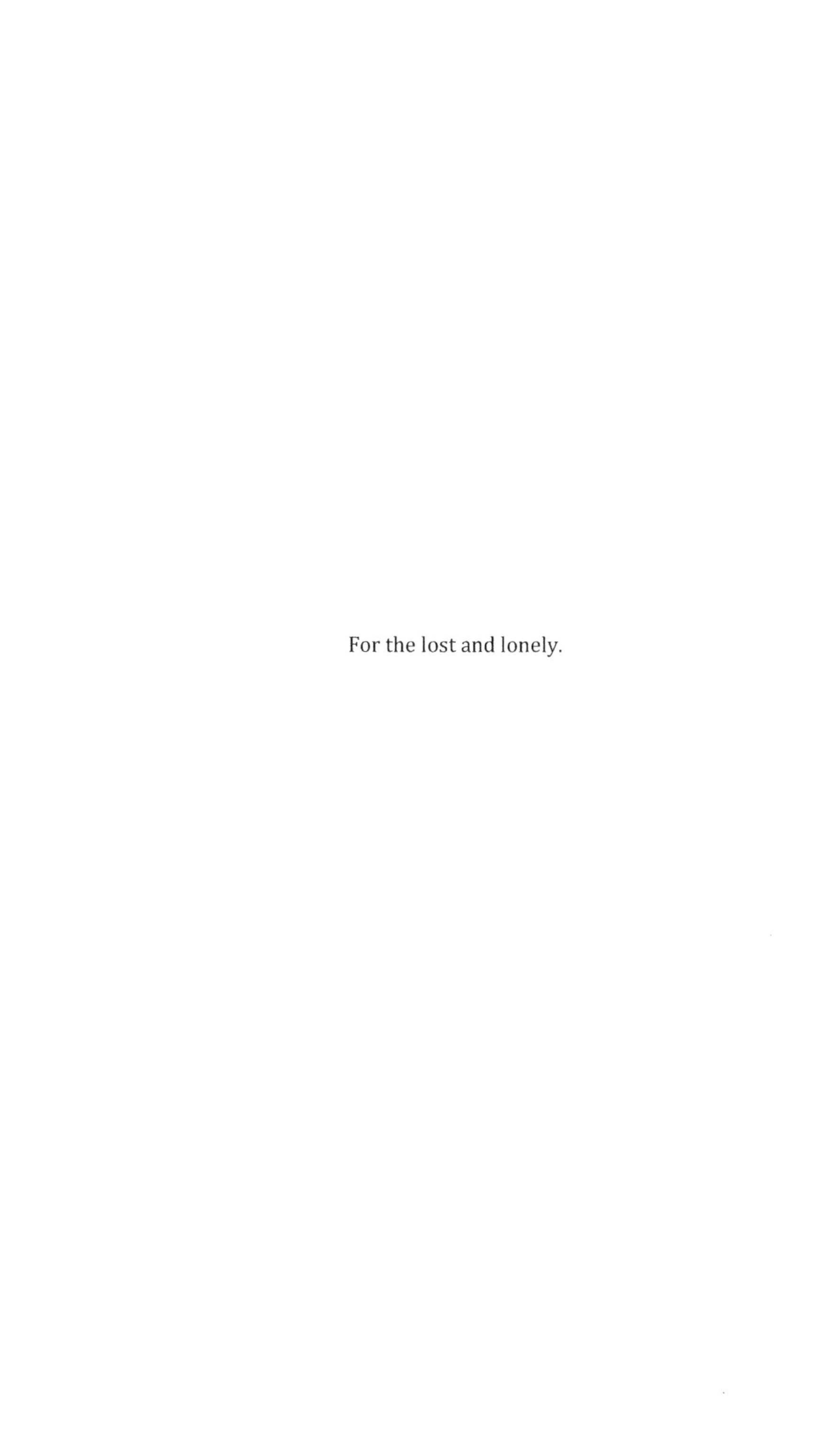

For the lost and lonely.

Hotel Ophelia

I.

Waking. Slowly at first. Then *bang-*

Back to earth. Back to life. To the heat and must and foist. As this relentless heatwave continues under a morning Yorkshire sun.

Through my window, mottled light - reds and yellows - filtered by a thick blanket curtain draped and taped across the double glazing, blackened by dried mildew. Alive with silverfish and woodlice. Frames drilled, screwed and painted so nothing can get in and nothing can get out. The dead curled into balls on the sill.

The papers are full of it. Hottest July since records began.

Ooh, what a scorcher! Britain Sizzles! says Emily, 18, from Plymouth. Brunette. Red and white polka-dot bikini. All nipples and freedom, sat in a municipal fountain. Made up wank-fodder for grease-monkeys and labourers. Scampering off to filthy bathrooms to knock one out behind busted plywood doors. Cum, scrunch and flush. Then back to the machines.

Lucy calls to me from the middle of the room surrounded by brittle sex tissues and greasy chip papers. Awake and alert. Poised, smooth and polished. Hard. Rising up from the chaos as my heart drums out an irregular beat, slowing down then speeding up. I'm at that age. I could go any second, leaving her to the mercy of the world and Logan Bone. So I sit and thank my God for another day of life and paradise.

Sometimes when I wake I forget why I'm here. Horror, then relief when I see her waiting in the blue shadows and it all makes sense. Hull and *The Cowley*. All this shit. While somewhere deep in the house Logan Bone crashes and curses, the thin walls shuddering with an unsteady half-drunk rage.

Pink piss-hole eyes unseeing like a new-born rat as he searches for the one-and-a-half litres of sickly screw-top plonk I hid last night - opened but not drunk - to mix with bootleg vodka and a dash of sherry. All sucked through a straw from a pink plastic water bottle like squash.

"You Fucking Cunt!", he yells in a smoked-out lung-rattle, wobbling like a marionette with imaginary puppet strings attached to his bony hands and yellow shit-covered fingers. All fag-stink and anger.

Looking at Lucy listening to Logan as a shy erection twitches beneath the tacky brown checked duvet cover, resting against the bare mattress.

I can smell him. Poppers, booze and breath. His dead man's face; slack wet lips and sunken eyes. Greasy grey tangles pulled back in a loose ponytail. Old pissy tracksuit bottoms, socks and sliders. A half-smoked Superking hanging from his lip as he begins his daily quest for oblivion. The morning shift at least.

My erection comes to nothing. Calf-muscles twitching from dehydration and poor diet. The usual summer sweats. Salts and minerals soaking the sheets and mattress, drying in rings. Dead skin feeding bugs and mites.

I've never seen Logan Bone eat. He has other appetites. Booze, drugs, boys. Young boys. Just kids. New to it. Looking for comfort and free chemicals. Laughing and cackling; gagging and gurgling; sucking and spanking. Then fighting, fearing injury and death; running back through the cluttered innards of the house in search of escape.

But I've never seen the mad fucker eat.

All night long. The chainsaw growl of dirt bikes outside our window. The slamming of car doors and blue smoke through headlamps as Logan Bone whispers into his black pay-as-you-go, credit low.

Except Logan Bone can't whisper. He's too caught up in it. Burrowed too deep into it. Into the soft earth of it. Shouting over himself to be heard.

Everything is urgent, and urgency is a clumsy beast. Banging around his head and house. Heavying his footsteps and the rattle in his chest beneath the old crispy skin covering his ribs and ringed baby-pink nipples.

Last night I found him passed out and piss-soaked. Belinda Carlisle on repeat on his giant multi-CD stack system in the lounge doubling as his bedroom because of the weed farm upstairs. So I hid his bottle in the washing machine because it haunts me too. His slow pointless life and death, as me and Lucy dream of better things away from the chaos. Just me and her.

Lucy's angry. Upset and rejected. Ignored and neglected. Annoyed at me for letting Logan get between us. Thinking of him when I should be thinking only of her. Kill him? He's killing himself. Be patient, I say, it's not forever.

That's why she's angry because she wants me all to herself. Immersed in her varnished flesh. Her hard machine-turned legs and wings; screws and runners. Her grain, unique like a fingerprint or a cell under a microscope.

I can draw it from memory. Every inch of her. Every line and swirl. All her patterns. Her appetite for me and my sex like nothing I'd ever encountered.

Every day like the first time. Coming together like animals, over and over before wiping her down with a damp J-cloth which I rinse and wring out daily in a kitchen sink full of filthy plates and bowls, and things that move and scuttle when disturbed before disappearing down the plughole.

Lucy's a pine dining table, and because she's a pine dining table she doesn't understand the world so I have to explain it to her. My daily transactions to keep us. What people do. What shops are. Babies. Other people. Dogs. The Wall. Chips. Logan Bone's unfortunate role in everything. But still, if it was up to her I'd never leave. And if it wasn't for food and work and water, I wouldn't either.

"Where's 'me fucking bottle?", whines Logan Bone through the door, twisting the handle.

"Fuck off Logan Bone!", I shout, my voice reverberating through the mattress springs like a conch shell held to my ear.

He's desperate, clinging on to vague memories, retracing his steps. This cycle of shame and repeat. Angry and violent like boiling water, hammering on the door then tiring as he claws lazily at the wood with long brown nails. I can feel his infant process as he thinks, his cheek and nose squashed flat, leaving oily smears and other traces on the paint. Trying to focus. Thinking and blinking. Get drug.

"Please Royal! The shop don't open 'til seven!"

Sammy the Paki won't serve him till he's got the boys out on their rounds. Logan knows that. Sammy doesn't mind serving drunks early but only after he's got the papers out. Half bottles of vodka or cans. Nothing big or bulky.

"I don't have it!"

"Well who the fuck does?", he growls, breaking character.

"You probably drank it!"

"I fuckin' didn't!"

He suddenly darkens. Becomes shadow. He's an addict. Everything's a short cut. Say what you need to say. Lie. Cheat. Steal. Efficient, like the flow of water. His wrinkled brow leaving a sweat mark the shape and size of a lamb's kidney on the door. Giant blocked pores. Eyes dead like a shark's. Red as a rabbit's.

Enough. Who cares? I've had my fun which wasn't any. Because there isn't any to be had. It's all out of necessity. Fun's for kids and the rich and the blissfully stupid. This is about money.

"It's in the machine", I scream from my side of the door.

"What fucking machine?"

"The fucking washing machine!"

"You said you didn't have it!", he moans.

"Well I lied!"

He punches the door like a child. No real intent. Just a rattle of knuckles. And off he fucks, bare feet on lino, gathering dust and grit and dusty gritty cat shit. Heel and toe. Bad knees and bunions. Then the distant metallic clicks and scrapes as he wrestles the broken door, gouging at the cracked scratched latch with a paint-flecked yellow-handled screwdriver from the drawer. Then nothing while he drinks, propped against the ancient Zanussi top loader.

Beige Artex swirls above me; the bare bulb; the cobwebs. Sudden footsteps – strong and confident - as he comes back for more. Emboldened by a few mouthfuls of cheap white fizz.

"Open the fucking door!", he shouts. His voice is strong.

"No!", I say.

But I have nowhere to go. No power. So I do as I'm told, naked from the waist down; a damp grey vest from the waist up. I'm taller and younger.

He's thin and weak and has stinking untreated ulcers on his legs wrapped in clingfilm and old bandages which he dries on a gas heater in the kitchen.

"Get out!", he spits jabbing the air with the screwdriver. "I've had enough of yous!"

"Me too", I say. Foolish words with consequences. The game we play. Have always played. It's all we have.

He looks through Lucy like she's not there. Like he doesn't care. Between her legs like they're nothing. As if she isn't the answer to everything.

"Then go!", he whines as he looks me up and down. Pure pantomime hatred.

He's so close. The stench of his breath. The black holes in his gums where his teeth used to be. Smears of white paste at each corner of his mouth, smacking his lips as smoke escapes from his huge hairy nostrils.

It's not just booze. It's chemical. Industrial chemical. Like a cleaning fluid wafting from him in an invisible mist. That and the smell of weed drifting down the stairs from the small Marijuana crop in the hot locked loft.

I imagine his pickled flesh and bones and bloated grey organs growing slowly into his guts.

I don't know why he asked me to stay. It was never discussed. But he brings it up when he's cross. Like it's his house. But it's not. It's a hand-out.

His name was on a list like everyone else's around here. Lists for this and lists for that. Lists for houses. Lists for food. Lists for money. Lists for help. And if it's not handed out it's stolen. The electricity jacked straight off the grid and everything else lifted off clothing rails and out of chill cabinets, or robbed straight out of people's houses.

But, yes, he took me in and gave me Lucy asking for very little in return. And I'm in his debt for that so I give him a bit here and there when I can. When I get shifts. Poke it under his bedroom door. We don't talk about it. We don't need to.

*

The house is silent now.

Logan Bone is thinking. Asleep or dead or thinking. But he's never dead. And he's not asleep. Every day he regains consciousness, puts on dry trousers and carries on where he left off. A vicious terrier looking for his next burrow to scramble down. Deeper and darker and dirtier than the last.

I take a piss, wiping myself on his stiff crusty flannel before putting it back where he keeps it, on top of the cabinet with some bath salts and a rusty razor. Sometimes I hide his toothbrush beneath the bath, prizing open the wobbly plastic side panel and tossing it amongst unimaginable spiders. Huge black things that move like mice.

All part of the game. Logan's not scared of spiders. Just himself. He wouldn't touch her. He's a coward. And Lucy would tell me. She understands human folly. I've told her everything. So I'd know if things weren't exactly as I left them or if he as much as touched her.

My factory fleece lies abandoned in the corner of the room. Misshapen. Inside-out. But it's something. I lick Lucy goodbye - grit on my dry white tongue; resistance on the sour varnish – and she smiles as I slip my hand between her legs, running my fat fingers along her rough hidden edges. Her notches and splinters and screw heads.

"See you later", I whisper. "I love you."

Don't go, she whispers back through the door. *Just a few more minutes. Come on. I thought you loved me.* She's teasing me. She always does this.

"I can't. I'll be late", I say playfully, open to offers, one hand on the door handle. But she doesn't push me. Because Logan Bone's listening, lurking on the other side of the door.

"See you later, I love you", he lisps in that mocking childlike whine of his as I lock the door behind me.

Phlegm rattle and cough. Then a sinister snarl. Drunk and calm. Like a mad spider who's been fed. "Don't worry. I'll look after her", grabbing his nuts through his tracksuit trousers. His sick bones against mine. A clumsy playground move with no real intent. He's not a fighter. He can barely stand, weak with his cancer and booze.

"You dare touch her", I say with a smile to appease him. But he doesn't smile back.

"And what? It's my fucking 'ouse. You can fuck off if you don't like it. Take that piece of shit with you."

I've heard it all before. The threats and ultimatums. Nothing to do but wait for nightfall and death. Whichever comes first.

Logan stands blinking like he can't think of anything. Like someone's turned him off.

"Suck my cock!", he finally stutters, spitting at my boots as I leave the house, his voice staying with me as I walk down the path.

Replaying it because there was something not right about it. Not just his tone but the look in his eye. Everything about him smaller, thinner and slightly weaker.

*

A 1996 Volvo 340. Brown inside and out. Different shades from deep shit to light rust. No badges, No trims. Worn mustard velour seats. An unstrung beaded seat cover chewing up thin upholstery and foam, spewing out spongey yellow flecks like crushed honeycomb.

Total shitheap.

The radio housing smashed and cracked; a mess of wires and circuit boards. A scentless green plastic turtle on a skateboard, stuck and re-stuck to the hide-effect vinyl dash with crispy Sellotape. The ashtray full of ancient fag ends and rock-hard pellets of chewed gum.

No tax. No MOT. No insurance. They don't check around here. Not on *The Cowley.*

Yellow polystyrene takeaway boxes fill the footwells and door pockets. Wooden forks. Ketchup sachets. Newspapers. Bent up twisted pop cans. Piles of rubbish, comforting and warm like animal bedding. If I could live in it I would, like a rat.

Somewhere no one will follow. Where Logan Bone can't go. And Lucy can't either. Because she doesn't have knees and her legs don't work or fold down or detach. Otherwise we'd pack up and go. But this is her home and she won't move, and I can't make her.

So I'm stuck and we stay, taking shifts at a food factory on an industrial estate about a fifteen minute drive from the estate. An area of reclaimed marshland linked to the rotting mainland by expressionless arterial roads and sudden cheerful roundabouts. Home to the countless huge beige metal sheds absorbing the relentless heat and light.

I park and shuffle through the carpark, an oily haze wobbling off the concrete.

Skips to my left, covered in blue, red and green tarps ready for filling and collection. The inevitable detritus of industry and processing. Cardboard and plastic and wood. Shattered pallets and binding. Raw materials shipped in, processed and shipped out in shiny plastic packets. A short fly-like life then sailed to landfill in barges. Buried and forgotten. Tomorrow's fossils.

There's a warm sickly waft of batter and pastry on an industrial scale. Repellent in this 33-degree heat. The prospect of eight hours tending a giant oven enough to drive you back to your dark damp cool burrow like a jungle spider.

But the people need their sweet potato wedges and mashed swede and apple pie, so we power through, to earn the money to buy our sweet potato wedges and mashed swede and apple pie and fags and drugs and booze and cheese and stolen flat-screens.

I'm tired of this. Living like this. The bits that don't involve her, to preserve the bits that do. Day in, day out. Over and over. On repeat. Reporting to the same security hut with twenty or so others - a rag-tag gang of silent sweaty miscreants with bad skin and terrible secrets.

Signed in and led through the turnstiles towards a rubberised changing room where we pull on white suits and boots and hair nets, policed by supervisors standing over us like camp commandants. A familiar drill and one that eats dignity. If you have any. Which no one does. Not here. And not on *The Cowley.*

One day they'll just line us up and shoot us. End the misery. Chop us up and pump our chum into the Steak & Kidney through the giant metal pipes, then hose away the blood and toss our bones in the skips. The ones covered by tarps to the left of the carpark as you walk in. Green, blue and red.

"Dean Dobbs. Jenny Head. Craig Biggs. Apple Pies. Red Section", says the woman at the front in her usual monotone without looking up from her clipboard as Dean, Jenny and Craig are led out of the portacabin over to the main plant. Walking to their daily death. The death of spirit.

You should have listened at school instead of wanking in the woods. Giving head in parked cars with a finger up your arse. Pissing it away in an act of stupid adolescent shit-thick defiance.

You should have listened but you didn't. You were too clever for that. Smoking weed in blacked-out Vauxhall Corsas, eyes like saucers. Thought you knew better. Like it would last forever. Or not thinking at all.

Thinking the day would never come. Well it has come and you're fucked. So think of that when you're pulling on your blue hairnet and packing up your pies and crumbles.

Crawling back to your hole in the ground, misery etched on your lost frightened Anglo-Saxon faces. Forever unable to smell baked apple and cinnamon without considering the rest of your unbearable fucking lives. The warm sickly smell of failure.

"Royal Warren?"

I hear but don't hear. I'm thinking about Lucy alone in the house. Imagining her legs. Beautifully symmetrical and bevelled. Running my hands up them until I'm leant against her with my cock out and all my weight on her polished top, spreading my buttocks and rocking her backwards and forwards as she begs for more.

Young, helpless, desperate.

"Royal Warren!?", she says again.

I raise my hand this time. I know where we're going. She's taking me to the machine.

*

16,000 hot Yorkshire puddings come at me every hour. Each one different. Each one the same. Rolling off in huge steel trays after the cook. Heat on heat.

My skin prickles as sweat drips down my flanks, face and legs, soaking my socks in these white rubber boots which squeak across the grippy concrete floors. Not that I can hear them over the nozzles and rollers and vast extractors preventing mass asphyxia.

My job; bin the burnt ones and the weird ones and the small ones. The rejects. Cripples and runts of the batter world. The ones no one wants. Children of a blocked nozzle.

They taste fine, just look wrong.

Because the machine isn't perfect either. She has inefficiencies and weak-points. Breakdowns and misfires. So I do what I'm told and rip her hissing, popping, squashed and deformed still-warm still-born spawn from her metal breast and condemn them to the maternity ward chute. Never to be spoken of again like a Victorian retard, all buck teeth and dribble.

My quick latex fingers, picking and flicking each under-par pudding into bright blue wheelie bins before they're taken outside and tipped into one of the large skips to the left of the carpark as you walk in, then sold as pig feed.

I have a responsibility to her - this one-stop Yorkshire Pudding machine and her 16,000-an-hour output, minus the flids - to listen and empathise. Soothe and comfort.

As she weeps for her dead babies through a symphony of clanks and cranks, squirts and spurts – the sound of thousands of individual components, bound by the lion-roar of eight giant extractors pumping her sickly vapour into the blue Yorkshire sky.

Because I'm the only one who'll listen. The only one who can see her and hear her. Growing closer and more intimate through each stage of the process as I wank in the batter and watch it slowly bake and rise under her heat.

Everyone else gets to go home and douse the flames of failure with booze, weed and dirty sex. But she's held prisoner. Pushed harder and faster and longer. Farmed like a backstreet Staffy bitch as replacement parts are shipped in from China and the Middle East to keep pace with production and the vicious demand for sugar and salt.

Half the estate works here. Whether it's Chips or Curly Fries or Lemon Meringue Pies or Sweet Potato Wedges. Yet it's our secret.

Logan Bone knows. Not about The Machine, no. Lucy. Spying through the keyhole. Watching my pale naked bulk slip and slide across her shiny flat pine top. So he keeps my secrets and I keep his. Like finding him unconscious with a courgette stuffed up his arse, or chaining young homeless kids to radiators, hands tied. Mouths stuffed with socks and cocks.

Technically Lucy belongs to him. She was already here. He pulled her out of a lock-up in Swansea delivering industrial sewing machines.

Took him all over until his legs got bad and he had to stop driving. They were throwing her out. He'd done his last drop, he said, and the van was empty, otherwise he would have left her behind and I'd be somewhere else.

Pine-topped. Rectangular. Slammed together in a workshop somewhere with a bunch of others. Knocked out. Her name carved into one of her legs in a jagged awkward heart shot with an arrow.

She's not like the machine. She communicates through stillness. The less she does the more she says. It's always been that way. After I first encountered Logan Bone outside that giant *Spoon's* in town screaming at passing cars through a traffic cone. Then back to *The Cowley* to his spare room, where I met Lucy and one thing led to another.

*

I had this recurring dream as a child. When I lived with my grandmother in the bungalow in Southend. Jumbled like dreams are, it went roughly like this:

My mother creeps into my room all dressed in black like a jewel thief, and raises a finger to her lips before ushering me out of bed and downstairs to the street where my half-brothers are waiting, sat on the low wall of the ornamental wishing well in my grandmother's front garden. We then tiptoe – the four of us – through the posh streets by the woods and the mansions overlooking the golf course. Single file, me at the back. Tim and Scott in the middle and my mother up front. My older brothers tell me to stay where I am and be lookout. To shout if anyone comes. Not to move from the spot under any circumstances or there'll be trouble. And I watch powerless as they climb the wall and disappear into the blackness of a huge back garden.

It's still and silent and the air is warm and I wait and wait but they don't come back. And I don't know what to do because I'm so young and so lost. And I don't know if they're still in the house or not. Or whether it's some cruel joke, or they're dead or they've been caught and taken away. So I wait by the wall and cry and hope they'll come back but they never do.

I don't know how many times I had that dream. Maybe just once. Maybe a thousand times. Maybe I didn't have it at all. But the story exists and I think about it often. The smell of my mother's perfume in the darkness. Polo mints and hairspray and the orange streetlights because no one dreams in pitch black.

But the panic was real, because I wake up with it still. And the horrific sense of being a child alone and abandoned in a terrifying world. I wake up with that too.

*

Wads of stuffing spill like guts from the squashed and mismatched sofas, stuffed back by lazy night cleaners. The grey-green walls rendered colourless by shadow. Two coffee tables covered in sugar and cold hot chocolate. Some fresh and wet. The rest old and dried. All from the coffee machine that doesn't dispense coffee and swallows your money 10p at a time if you're stupid enough to try.

On the sofas lounge five workmen in steel-toed leather rigger boots. Legs wide, itching their nuts. Watching porn on smashed smartphone screens, as they eat wafer-thin ham sandwiches and cold multi-pack pasties.

No zero-hour contracts for them. Part of the drab crushed furniture. With paid holidays and workplace pensions and job security not afforded to the rest of us. Sitting around the edges of the room like we don't exist. Marked out by our purple temp fleeces and white wellingtons. All hail the five.

One holds up his phone as a signal to gather. Then whoops of laughter as their sandwiches and pasties become visible thick white paste on tongues, teeth and gums. Specks and globs, spraying wet bread and saliva onto the dislodged carpet tiles.

I watch from the corner. The ebb and flow. Reacting how they think they should. How Murph wants them to. His red cheeks and ginger beard. Chinese tattoos on flabby biceps. Powerful and violent when pushed.

He points at me. "You seen this?"

I ignore him and carry on eating my chips from the van outside.

"Oi, I'm talking to you!", he barks, waving me over.

"I'm alright", I say blushing, fear and discomfort revealed in a brief awkward squint.

"I'm not going to fuckin' ask you again!"

No option, so I give in and go, kneeling beside him on the hard floor. It's three-and-a-half minutes long. Grainy handheld footage of a pale 60-year-old woman in red stockings and suspenders and full-length black satin gloves, sucking off a black Great Dane in what looks like a 1980's ski chalet. Videotaped, digitised and uploaded.

She manoeuvres herself uncomfortably for the lens feigning ecstasy as thick drool hangs from the giant dog's wet jowls; thirsty, anxious and confused.

I smile and give Murph back the phone but he pushes it back to me, right into my face until I can feel the cold screen against my hot red cheek.

"All of it", he says as the dog ejaculates, directing a hot jet of Great Dane spunk onto her face and neck. In her eyes, round her mouth, in her hair. Her face suddenly registering the full terrifying horror of what she's just done for money, as the spunk cools and runs between her small pale tits.

"Hmmmmmmm... good doggy", she groans, licking her lips and flicking her tongue over the glistening dog dick.

She's a shit actress. Maybe that's why she's there. Explored all other avenues. Casting after casting. No after no, until rejection and loneliness took their toll. Then a journey through addiction from booze to smack via coke and speed, into strip clubs and strip club carparks, then human porn before she got too old and found herself in a category of one.

Sucking off animals to pay the rent. Paid in cash with the promise of constant work. Hopefully she's got dementia by now and forgotten all about it, sat shitting in a giant nappy in some sleepy Bavarian nursing home. Or just plain dead. RIP.

"He's got a fuckin' stiffy!", screams one of the factory cunts.

"You dirty fucker!", grunts Murph.

"Dirty fuckin' dog nonce", says his mate, filming me as I go back to the corner to my cold chips and shame as the siren sounds for the afternoon shift.

*

"Don't worry about that lot earlier. They're idiots", says a man called Terry as we walk back across the carpark.

He opens his boot and perches on the rubber seal to change into some old trainers. "What you doing the weekend?"

"Stopping in", I say. I have nothing to change into. I just want to get back to Lucy. I don't want to talk to him. There's a silence.

"I'm taking the boys to see their Nan. She's not doing so well. Doubt she'll last that much longer."

I didn't ask and I don't care.

He's older than us. Cares about his job. Works hard to cling on. Has a clear plastic crate where he lays his work boots after brushing the dust off them with a brush neatly labelled 'CAR'.

Organised and precise. Takes pride. Which makes it worse. At least we don't care. At least we're not happy. At least our presence here is just part of the filthy chaos and complex misery of everything else. Whereas Terry seems content, which doesn't make any sense.

Because this shouldn't be enough for anyone.

*

Logan Bone smashes the lock with a lump hammer and stands staring at the table with eyes never before seen. Sweating heavily and muttering under his breath. Drinking all day. Playing it all back. Getting it all tangled up. Remembering it wrong, over and over.

Total conviction. There are voices. Different ones. The smoke tastes strange on his tongue, feels strange in his lungs. He's had enough. He's tired. Tired of this long slow inevitable death.

"Piece of shit! ... Fucking fuck!"

He pulls it towards the door revealing four perfect circles of flat clean green carpet pile. Shafts of cheap sunlight picking out dust and fibre as he drags it down the dank passage, angling the legs through the doorway. Then through the dogleg, gouging the graffitied textured wallpaper with its sharp corners. There's a shooting pain in his arthritic fingertips but he only has to do it once. He can't change his mind. He can't go back.

This is it.

"... fuck with mine, I'll fuck with yours..."

Why not him? Why Royal? Who anointed fucking Royal? Fat fucking useless piece of shit Royal. Which God? Why did the divine light of true love shine on him when Logan had been searching his whole life?

What made ugly fat fucking Royal so special? He took him in. Gave him a bed. Gave him that fucking table. Didn't lay a finger on him. Not a finger. Let him stay till he sorted himself out. Thought nothing of it till Royal started acting strange, jizzing all over it and wiping it down with his socks and the cloths under the sink.

So where was his? Where was his love and joy? His stillness. His reason to exist.

Logan Bone hadn't always been like this. He'd mutated out of something good having lost a love of his own.

A loss he couldn't process or understand. And as his heart rested and healed, he fell into the gap between grief and madness where he stayed. Unable to get back. A one-way door.

Why do bad things happen to good people? he wondered. A thought that consumed him until he forgot who he really was and his body and mind slowly failed, revealing the Logan Bone they knew.

Tolerated and celebrated by a community happy to smoke his weed and toss coins in his bucket in return for the show.

He can feel the tumour in his guts, grinding against the table top as its wooden legs bang and scrape down the steps onto the path.

When it was quiet he could hear it, he thought. Gnawing at his bones and blood and organs. The pop and fizz of erosion. Killing tissue. Turning everything black. An inside job while Royal had love and serenity.

He held that table responsible for his sickness, like a cursed death mask or haunted relic. He wished he'd never brought it home.

Down the sideway he scrapes out a half-smoked cigarette, lifts the green tarp and reaches for a petrol can as scores of woodlice panic and scatter. Then drops it so the contents spill onto the worn turf soaking his socks and shorts and greasing his hands as the fumes fill his head with stars and dots.

"Fuck!", he mutters, short of breath.

He picks it up, dousing the table. Double-dousing. Making sure. One for luck. Stars and dots. Splish, splosh. A little more. Stars and dots. Greasing and soaking, greasing and soaking. Light-headed, he fumbles for the matches all thumbs and knuckles, and opens them upside-down so they tumble onto the scorched earth. Stars and dots, stars and dots.

Pause. A momentary flashback to childhood and innocence. Sanity. A performance. Christmas. A cold church hall. Waiting backstage. The smell of incense. His mother and father in the audience. Butterflies and nerves. A desperate desire to please.

God he missed them.

*

The Wall.

A raised flowerless rectangle of baked dirt and fag ends enclosed by bricks. A magnet for drunks, scumbags and thieves, opposite a parade of six shops.

Whatever you want, whatever you need. Cheap booze. Fake fags. Stolen meat and cheese. School shoes. Laptops. Phones. Drugs obviously. There and then, or within the hour at a price. All on tick, because ends don't meet on *The Cowley*. Never have, never will.

'*... and don't go near The Wall!*' yelled generations of mums to their kids as they ran out of small terraced houses hunting fun and trouble. Maybe theirs would make it off the *The Cowley*; make something of their lives. Finish school. Get some exams. A job in an office maybe. But they had to stay away from The Wall. Because no good had ever come from it.

The queue in the chippy's longer on Fridays. Those fat mum's getting fatter. Dirty toddlers sucking fistfuls of sodden Wotsits.

Outside, a group of boys doing stunts on mountain bikes, clattering over a jump made of bricks and MDF.

They know me, the old boy and his wife. Greek immigrants in their sixties, and their Downs Syndrome daughter who clears tables and washes up with a constant smile.

There's a framed Greek flag screwed to the wall and various printed water colour sunsets hanging in black plastic frames. Cheap trinkets and souvenirs. Dolls in plastic tubes, sticky with years of grease.

"Fucking kids", whispers the old boy as he stirs the bubbling oil. Poor bastard. He shouldn't have to put up with this shit. We should. It's our shit. But it's not his shit. Why would you choose this shit? Born here, fine. That's not a choice. But him and the old girl and the daughter? They should be at home looking out over the Aegean or something, not The Wall.

Two teenage girls sit at the Formica-topped table nearest the window below the words 'Fish & Chips' reverse sign-written on the glass in an arc.

Fourteen or fifteen. Painted nails and thick pink lipstick. The smell of cheap perfume and vinegar. The start of a long night, kicking around the dusty estate. Rolling the dice, unsure where it will lead. Maybe back to The Wall or The British Queen, a portacabin estate pub with dead hanging baskets, razor wire and an Alsatian on the roof.

Cadging drinks and disappearing with strangers. Two's up. Free coke and MDMA. Getting spit-roasted on a cream leather sofa surrounded by oily motorbike parts on newspaper and crates of bulk-bought dog food. Who knows? But there'll be no fairy tale ending. Not here. Not tonight. Not ever. Not on *The Cowley.*

Watching me through thick black lashes, kicking each other under the table. The one facing me, blonde and sharp, spreading her legs so I can see her knickers and pubic hair.

"If you like fish, mate", she shrieks waving her fingers in the air before licking them like a lollypop. "Dirty fucker!"

Call me dirty fucker you little slag. Just like your mum and her mum before. The family business. Using youth and flesh as currency. But give it ten years. Ten years of Sweet Potato Wedges and stolen cash 'n' carry cheese. Then we'll see. As you queue for chips with your shitty kids rolling around in the dirt and dogshit at your dry cracked feet. Topping up at the foodbank midweek while you try and remember what it felt like to be that girl in the window with something to sell. Then we'll see.

"£1.70", says the old woman, sliding the chips across the counter. "Sauce?"

"No."

She always asks but there's ketchup in the car. And as the girls lick their teeth and giggle I can hear sirens and look up as a thin column of smoke drifts into a clear blue sky behind a row of identical grey council houses.

A tire probably, or a bin.

*

Logan Bone lies burnt to death in a pool of muddy water, Lucy at his side. Smouldering remnants. Wood, flesh, ash and hot brackets.

Thoughts flash. The smell of a petrol, cooked meat and burnt plastic. This will take years. Whatever this is. If it's what I think it is. She's never coming back. I'll never get to hold her and kiss her and fuck her. This is for life. Forever. Nothing will ever be the same.

A sudden nausea at the horror of what's laid out before me tingles in the back of my throat and cheeks. I'm giddy and slump, looking up at the grotesque spinning green faces. The police holding them back. The mob. The entire laughing, baying, screaming, crowing Cowley.

"That's enough,... come on ....stand back! GET BACK!", says a policeman.

Why aren't they helping? Why aren't you helping? Why didn't you stop him? Let him burn.

Logan Bone's clothes are fused to him, skin gone. His face, gone; Head, red and hairless like a skinned Chimpanzee curled up glistening in the sun. The wet earth and grass scorched black as run-off gurgles in the gutters, taking surface dust and fag butts with it.

The same contorted expression, even in death. Just a different pain as his skin blistered and his clothes melted. Stiff hands frozen in time like a Pompeii peasant.
I feel a momentary gladness that his suffering is over. Then it's gone. Because she's dead too and that mad fucker killed her. Lying before me on the grass - blackened, silent and wet.

I claw at the earth, covering myself in her charred remains. Slimy, warm and gritty. Under my nails. In my mouth. That taste of bonfires and sulphur and mud. The day after bonfire night. Craving physical pain to make some sense of the stinging confusion of shock, grief and disbelief. Seeking out heat to create something permanent, gripping tightly onto the embers until my bare hands blister.

If only I could be with her. If only Logan Bone had killed us both. Strapped me to her and taken us together as our very different bodies were destroyed by the same fire.

It's not true, says the optimist. *She's dead*, says the truth. *Everything's dead*, says the pessimist.

Behind me tires slow and doors slam as I smear myself in her warm remains. Footsteps and the metallic clink and snap of a gurney.

I can't start again. I need to die. It's a crushing moment. I've wanted to be dead before but now I need it. Soak me in whatever that was. Hit me with a spade. Shoot me. Cut my throat. Gouge my heart out and feed it to the pigs.

They're laughing. Taking pictures. Texting and filming. Facebook stars. Me and Logan Bone. Dead and Alive. Cooked and Raw. Fat and thin. While fish fingers and peas go cold on dinner tables and TV's play to empty front rooms. Shirtless men drinking cans. Fuck the police. Fuck Logan Bone. This is it. Summer. We were there. The day he burned. Friday night LOLs. As long as it's someone else they're happy. But their time will come. One day it'll be them.

Hands pull at my shoulders, and I look up into a friendly face haloed by the sinking sun.

"Come on, love", she says, all dressed in green. "Let's have a look at that hand. What's your name, love?"

"Royal", I say.

"Royal? As in … the Queen?"

"Yes", I say. "Is that your first name?", she asks.

"Yes."

"And what have you been doing today, Royal? Have you been at work?"

"Yes."

"I thought I recognised that jumper. My cousin's a forklift driver over there. What do you do love?"

"Yorkshire puddings", I say. Then, "She's dead."

"Who's dead, love?" There's a sudden urgency in her voice.
"Lucy."

"Who's Lucy?"

"My wife."
"She's right here!", I say thrusting my hands into ashes and embers.

"So there's no one inside the house, Royal? Just to be clear."

"She's here!" I take a handful of ash and offer it as proof. "He killed her", I say, pointing at Logan.

There's a pause while she professionally assesses the degree of risk, glancing briefly at her partner then back to me.

"Let's pop you in the back of the ambulance, love", she says sympathetically, helping me to my knees, steadying me. One foot in front of the other like a drunk. One shoe. Wet clothes. Burns and blisters and blue flashing lights. *Oohs* and *Ahs*. The constant laughter. A circus. A street party.

I glimpse a fluorescent yellow boob tube and the girl from the chip shop staring at me like she knows everything. I can smell her cheap sweet perfume.

"You dirty fucker", I whisper, stepping up into the ambulance.

II.

Half a kilometre off the south-east Essex coast Alma hauls herself out of the freezing sea onto the floating pontoon and waits for the approaching splutter of a fibreglass tender to die in the fog.

Seven feet, tail to crown, with long black hands and fingers. Her skin green and waxy, scabbed and raw. She flops onto the platform with a wet thud, pulling the package up after her, lit by the three-quarter moon and the strings of multi-coloured bulbs lining the old pier.

The pontoon rocks gently, then violently then gently again. The wash from a bigger vessel long since gone, like light from a dead star. Not far away a trawler rumbles unnoticed through the mist, back from its fog-bound pick-up deep in the cockle fields.

"Where have you been?", she hisses at the awkward silhouette of a woman, as she moors the tender to a barnacled oil drum.

"I got held up", says the woman gruffly, stepping into the light and transferring her weight from one vessel to the next as Alma shifts onto her front and props herself up on her palms like a seal. Layer upon layer of dull scales reflecting the moonlight as her weakened muscles flex and roll under her thick hide.

Coco's wearing a sheer dress and stockings and thick make-up on her face and lips. Hands on hips. Her perfume overwhelms Alma, her sense of smell many times keener than a humans.

"Did you bring any fags?"

Coco lights a cigarette and places it between Alma's thin blue lips. There's an audible crack of scales as Alma inhales and ribbons of smoke escape from her gill slits and nostrils.

"Did anyone see you?"

"Fuck you", Alma whispers, scales creaking with displeasure.

Coco hands her a half-bottle of bad brandy, stepping towards her as she drinks, pulling up her dress, naked underneath. Alma maintains eye contact as her long black tongue flicks in and out. She knows what Coco likes. She's drunk. She can feel it in Coco's legs and buttocks as she pulls hard on Alma's wet matted hair, freezing cold and full of silt.

She feels briefly wanted. The warmth of Autumns. She remembers how it used to be. Centuries past. Dancing with ghosts and beasts. Beauty and innocence. Corrupted now. Washed up in this shithole provincial forgotten town with a habit and a chronic skin disease that won't heal.

Her and the others. Just junkies chasing fixes. They had the connections. That was easy. Same as before. Pirates and thieves. Smugglers and dealers selling escape. They knew these waters better than the fishermen. The magic in the darkness, hiding in the deep. Yellow teeth and eyes. The things no one saw or thought existed. When it was fun. When they ran it like a business, controlling the shipping lanes and remote coastlines and coves.

Negotiating with the land and the small-time crooks that ran it. Skimming their cut in return for barrels and watertight boxes safely stored and delivered on time.

Then the patrol boats appeared and the smugglers headed north to Suffolk and Norfolk and everything died. Demand outstripping supply as desperation set in.

Now they took what they could. Did what they had to do. Everyone wants to fuck a mermaid. People will fuck anything.

It was alright for them with their mortality and limited life expectancy. But this girl needed to make a living.

Coco loads a metal gauze with crystals and hands it to her and she inhales until her brain swims with nausea and warmth. Like love but safer. Love. She smiles. Where did it go? Him. She loves him. Her, whatever. God, yes. But she knows what that love is. Enmeshed with loneliness and chemical dependence and regret. She loves Coco because that's all there is. And because she asks her how she is, and kisses her when she needn't.

"I need to get back. Things to do", she says, taking back the pipe and the package.

"Stay a bit longer", Alma says, but Coco ignores her like she always does. One day. She's got what she came for. Alma lies back on the freezing deck as thoughts spill from her head; dreams of sunsets and whale-bones and crystal meth as she rolls back into the water and sinks slowly to the bottom, forgetting briefly who, where and what she is.

*

Swan House is a small private psychiatric hospital near Beverley. Backing onto woods and part hidden by conifers, sitting back from the road and the passing through-traffic. Only the painted sign gives it away as anything other than a large family house at the end of a gravel driveway. But inside it's a hospital. Twelve single hospital bedrooms – all similar in size with a metal hospital bed, wardrobe and small chest of drawers, and a separate toilet, basin and shower in an *en suite* wet room. Windows bolted shut and help never far away. Just pull the chord or hit the button.

Kate-28 scrubs at a sheet of paper with a blunted purple felt-tip pen, her eyes black and blank behind the greasy fringe she cuts herself. Page after page. Hour after hour. Like a broken Yorkshire Pudding machine or porridge pot that can't stop.

Scratching and squeaking with mute screams as they give her fresh reams and count the days until she disappears off to her next botched attempt at independent living. Delivered back bandaged and bound in a community ambulance, stopping briefly at Ryman.

I gave her the name to make her mine. More mine than everyone else's. She's like some complicated android from space. A robot with feelings. A human without.

Maybe that's why I like her. She's another broken machine performing one simple action over and over as her faulty wires and receptors fizz and pop.

On the other side of the room sits Aaron, draped over an armchair like dry-cleaning. Pale scars zig-zag his forearms and wrists. Just a child. Dulling a pain that isn't his. The cycle of neglect and abuse. Just a kid. Addicted to THC. Cap and trainers. Floppy and boneless. Pale and empty.

Two chairs up Seamus trades life stories for pity. His giant buttocks spread across two seats, working ancient high street loafers off holed odd socks, heel and toe. Big fat Seamus and his big fat arse and his big fat mouth. Always flapping. Foaming and spitting. Talking to no one, anyone. Ego wrestling low self-esteem and winning for now, as he rolls tiny fags in his rock hard redundant bricklayer's fingers.

I told the police everything. How me and Logan ended up living in the same house. How I first met Lucy. The empty Lambrini bottle in the washing machine. His habits and his sickness. Things I'd seen and heard around the house.

It all pointed to misadventure. A revenge crime or psychotic episode exacerbated by booze and drugs and various chronic personality disorders. Suicide was ruled out. He wasn't trying to kill himself, he was just arseholed in charge of a petrol can.

Then they told me I couldn't go back. The house wasn't his to give. My name wasn't on anything official. No bills or lists or documents. Even though that room had made me happier than I'd ever been. It was witness to our marriage. Witness to our most intimate moments. It was part of it all. But in the cold daylight of official bureaucracy all that meant nothing.

So I cried and walked for two days and two nights with nowhere to go, sleeping under some cardboard boxes behind B&Q before jumping off a pedestrian bridge into the bus lane of an underpass in town, landing on the roof of a park-and-ride before bouncing onto the tarmac below. So they brought me here and dressed my wounds while they worked out who to blame. Which department? Who failed me most? Trying to locate the exact crack I fell through. Another mental health statistic to cover up and shuffle along. I've never generated revenue for this country and never will.

My face is healing. Just scabs and tenderness around my chin and neck. Heart, broken. Not burnt or blistered, just broken. My only function now to shit and piss and sweat and breathe and sleep and harbour painful memories. No rent to pay. No addiction to feed.

Nothing and no one to love. A heart beating for no reason. Abandoned to Cash In The Attic and Loose Women from an old velveteen recliner in this grim dim dayroom.

There are pink marks on the fabric. Dried hard. Calamine lotion or Pepto Bismol. A previous life for the chair and its mismatched step-brethren. A hotchpotch of reclaimed sofas, footstools and cushions pushed together in an arc around an old box TV on a bowed bracket, revealing red Rawl plugs and lint and a barely unnoticeable build-up of pale pink dust on the skirting board several feet below.

A warm oily bath of Denise Welch and David Dickinson in saturated technicolour, stretched at the edges, where people sit and talk and cheer and clap and win and lose. Where the stakes are low and everyone goes home with something.

Where red and yellow T-shirts out-boot fair each other and IT consultants answer multiple-choice questions for money on garish neon sets. Their 15 minutes plus the ad breaks. Those less desperate than us. Still functioning. *...I came with nothing and I left with nothing...*

(No Alan, you left with much less now a modest daytime TV audience knows you think Reykjavik's in Denmark).

But my clothes smell fresh, there's fish on Fridays and bedtime is a pill. I don't know what else they're putting in me. I don't care. It's a free bar. You take what you can then get your head down. Multi-coloured tablets in small waxed paper cups. Form an orderly queue and wait for your peace.

There's still pain. But it's someone else's pain. Like I'm watching it on that old screen, or having it explained to me so it doesn't really resonate. I crave real pain. I want to miss her. I want it to hurt. I want the ache and the sting and the choke. At least I think I do. it. But I can't mourn because the drugs won't let me. I guess I'm easier to marshal with my heart safely inside my body.

So I consume with dry eyes and express nothing. More interested in Peter Andre's latest half-child with his latest child-wife in the latest instalment of his incredible celebrity half-life. Updated daily.

Does Peter live episodically? Does something happen to him every day? Does he have to feel certain things at certain times? Does he exist at all? So many questions.

Seamus rants all the way through Bargain Hunt. They've given him a date.

"…I can't fuckin' go home… home to fuckin' what?... home's the fuckin' reason I'm here… …. you try living eight to a fuckin' room on ninety-fuckin'-quid a week… I'll do it again... make fuckin' sure this time…. I'll cut my own fuckin' throat… they don't fuckin' care about no one … they'd rather I was fuckin' dead… it's all about the fuckin' money…."

"Shut the fuck up Seamus. No one gives a fuck", says Osman.

Osman hasn't seen his children since his wife took them back to Egypt. Says he's in exile and can't go home because he's ex-Special Forces and got caught up in the uprising. It was that or execution. Then his wife ran off in the middle of the night under state pardon and took the kids with her.

So he attached a hosepipe to the exhaust of his Mondeo Zetec and went to sleep with a picture of the children in his mouth before a dogwalker found him and pulled him out. That's suffering. Not the Seamus kind. The selfish kind. Anyone can stop drinking. Anyone can not start again.

"What the fuck did that cunt say to me? What did you say to me cunt?", screams Seamus.

"I say people are trying watch the fuckin' television", says Osman.

He looks around for support but there isn't any.

"I'll say what I want in my own fuckin' country. You want to listen to the fuckin' television, fuckin' turn it up."

"You're Irish", mutters Kate-28.

She doesn't speak often but when she does, *boy-o-boy.*

Seamus's face reddens. Victim. I can see it now. The child. Always in trouble. Drunkenly beaten with dogma.

"Are you listening to this?", he says. "The Egyptian thinks he makes the fucking rules. That's where we're at in this fuckin' country. Fuckin' Africans. You're not in Egypt now, son. You're fucking with the Irish!"

"Shut up Seamus", I say.

"What?", he says.

I've heard enough. Had enough. I don't care about Osman. I care about Cash in the Attic and silence and justice. I care about what's right. I care about love. I don't care about Seamus. We all have problems. That's why we're here. Because we're shit at living. Shit at putting one foot in front of the other, paying bills and blocking out pain. And shit at dying, in my case.

But I do care about Kate-28 and her purple felt-tips and her wonderfully achievable ambitions. I want to be in there with her. See what she sees. I could do it on these drugs. Whatever they are. I could love her and she could love me. Her voice, new and soft.

"And what the fuck's it got to do with you?", screams Seamus, a cry in his voice. This is new to him. Resistance.

"You've got your date so shut up", I say. Seamus has gone unanswered for too long. We all have. It has to go somewhere. The rage. And the pain and suffering. You can't just drug it out of us. It doesn't work like that. So it ignites like fuel vapours.

Be careful Royal, screams Kate-28 deep in my imagination. This moment of adversity has made her see. Shaken her awake. She's noticed me. Medication and all. I love you too.

Then Seamus is on me, crushing me. I can smell his breath and skin – fags and tea and tooth decay – sweating rage and swinging blindly at my head and face with fat fists.

I free myself and rush at his huge thighs, knocking him off balance. But he's strong and he clamps a fat unwashed forearm around my neck and runs the top of my head at the wall with a muted crack as the brackets finally give in and eight kilograms of 1987 box TV falls screen-down on the back of his head. The end of the fight, if you could call it that. And the end of Seamus as he curls into a sobbing ball, all flab and arse-crack.

"I'm sorry! I'm fuckin' sorry!", he whispers, blood and snot soaking his shirt. He's been doing this all his life. Lashing out and losing. No second-chances. This is why he's where he is. Whiskey and anger. Blood in his eyes.

"It was all me! It's always me!" The words choke him. All part of the play. Blaming what he's become. Negotiating forgiveness. But it's too late. Seamus is on his way. He's fucked up again. Barred from another pub. Barred from another nuthouse. Surely he's running out of places to go. Self-death still his only real chance of freedom.

Bernie appears at the door as a klaxon sounds throughout the building. "Everyone to the dining room - now!"

I struggle to my feet, covered in dust and glass.

"Not you", he says.

*

Helen slides her notes to one side. Bernie sits beside her, shoulders hunched, staring straight down at some notes with his on his lap or his knees, I can't see.

She's big. Clumsy. Strangely tall and wide-hipped, wearing high-waisted bootcut black jeans and a baggy brown jumper. Her face and chins framed by an unflattering mousy bob. Alone, I'd imagine. A kind mask disguising whatever isn't right. An all too frequent hangover possibly. Loneliness perhaps. Tedium almost certainly.

UPVC double-glazed windows look out over yellow wheelie bins in a small untidy recess next to the kitchen. Beside them a porter sucks on his cigarette, slowly yet thoughtfully moving away when our eyes meet. Inside meets outside. Mental meets normal. Either he's ashamed or thinks I should be.

Helen takes a sideway glance at my notes looks up.

"How are you feeling?"

I don't answer her, staring instead at the bins and the bright white sky through the nets.

"Anything you want to talk about since last week, Royal?"

"Not really."

"Any negative thoughts? Suicidal thoughts?"

The kitchen hand moves briefly back into view to stub out his cigarette on a concrete ledge before going back inside. "No thoughts of self-harm, or low mood?"

"I don't feel anything."

"The medication is there to stabilise you", she says.

"I miss her", I say.

"That's understandable. But you're feeling better about things generally, which is really good progress."

"Understandable to me, but it's not understandable to you."

"And why do you say that Royal?"

"Because no one knows how I'm feeling apart from me."

"Have you been filling out your mood sheet?"

"Fuck the mood sheets, Helen."

I'm different with her. Nasty. She annoys me. He manner. Her weaknesses. We're all different with different people. She makes me want to speak and swear.

Helen composes herself, preparing a response as Bernie glares at me across the table wringing his hands. "You seem angry, Royal. Why are you angry?"

"Because we have this conversation every week. I'm bored of talking about it. It doesn't change anything."

She shuffles uncomfortably in her chair, eyebrows raised like something bad is about to happen. Bernie looks up.

"What happened with Seamus?", he says.

"He was upsetting Kate."

"You know we can't tolerate violence under any circumstances", he says.

And suddenly this little tag team makes sense. It's over. They're going to throw me out. Or lock me further away. Deep in the vaults. It's coming. I can feel it. A smaller, harder, more secure hospital on an island out of view. Maybe that's how this thing works. No one knows I'm here. No one knows I'm not here.

What is clear is no one wants me here. No one ever has.

"I wasn't being violent", I say.

"Seamus says you started it", says Bernie, Helen's contribution reduced to mute observer.

She was just opening for him. The fucking warm-up act. They're circling. Looking for my weak points. Tiring me out like Orcas do a seal.

These constant questions. This constant dialogue. That and the drugs. The multi-coloured pills in the waxed paper cups. It solves nothing. Achieves less. I don't want to talk. I want to colour like Kate-28. I just don't have the pens or the paper or the discipline.

"He would. He's fighting for his life", I say but it falls on deaf ears.

They're going to kill me, or worse keep me alive.

*

The bus and the underpass were just farce. Ill thought out. Poorly executed. Pathetic. I don't think I even wanted to die. I just wanted something to happen. Some drama. But this is different. More measured. Full circle, from Essex along the coasts and edges into countryside and city back again to my place of birth. Sleeping between the joists in building sites in Cricklewood and Vauxhall. Mile End Cemetery. Picking fruit through Kent. Sleeping on benches and beaches in Rottingdean and Bournemouth.

Then Plymouth, where I met the Frazers, and on to Clifton to steal copper and camp in the railway arches drinking rainwater, spatchcocking rabbits. On the fly. Hand to mouth. Finally Hull and Logan Bone and *The Cowley*.

Now just me and a mute locum in a small patch of woodland in North Yorkshire. One step at a time, as my blood absorbs much needed oxygen and my flesh turns lipstick red from its usual purply-grey.

I asked Kate-28 to go with me but she didn't answer. Just carried on colouring. Didn't even look up. My impotent fantasy simply that. Her handing me my medal in that Throne Room, flirting and smirking, as we confront our feelings. Pure fiction.

For a split-second I thought we could save each other. But I was wrong. So I asked Afzal to take me for a walk in the woods. Then said I needed a piss and watched as he pulled his phone out of his anorak pocket, crouching by a rotten log too wet and mossy to sit on. Instantly and totally immersed in his digital wonderland while I pissed slowly and loudly then ran as fast as I could, hard and straight like a rhino towards the insulated rumble of A-road traffic bouncing back through the trees and branches.

A beast crashing clumsily for its life - or in this case death – as Afzal's panicked voices chased me through the trees, dampened by waist-high bracken.

"Royal! Royal! Roy-al!"

It was strange hearing it. He'd never called me by my name before.

III.

It was hot when I left in the back of the ambulance. Oven hot. Machine hot. The air fat with chatter and excitement as bottles of booze and loft-grown weed went up and down The Wall. The people were happier. Life was better, or so it seemed. Summer does that.

Tinny dance anthems on tiny speakers and smart phones. Every muddy patch of grass scorched brown by the warrior sun. Long shadows and everything brushed magic-gold as the kids made sticky associations of happiness. They'll remember that summer forever, some of them. Times they'll wish they could have back as they're sucked further and further down like paralysed rats into the belly of the snake.

Now it's grey and damp and cold. Hard shoulders hunched against the wind and rain as they hustle and deal. On the make and rob. No gold. No magic. Hope gone. Blowbacks in piss-stinking stairwells. Playing the blame-game as they burgle and fiddle, stealing nappies, cheese and phones. Stuff they can sell. Stuff people need but can't afford for cash or drugs, or sex if things are slow. Some will do anything to feed their kids.

On the field down from The Wall there's the normal scattering of dead fires and sodden mattresses, rusting supermarket trolleys and splintered milk-crates. Anything you can lob or break or destroy. Render useless and unfit for purpose. Wheels off. Screens smashed. Forks and frames bent out of shape. Arcing high in the air before falling back to wet earth.

A mini-motorbike buzzes and putters right to left as some kids make a jump from a salvaged shop fascia and bricks. Human erosion. The field and The Wall and their front gardens and homes. Each other. Eroding and abrading. Grinding it down. Grinding it up. Like stones on a beach as they become sand then silt.

I feel a pang of fondness for it. But I'm on a different orbit now. The universe knows that, even if the people don't.

The house stands boarded up and graffitied. Perforated steel panels drilled into the walls and padlocked shut. 'DO NOT ENTER' and 'TRESPASSERS WILL BE PROSECUTED' signs from a private security firm. The word 'PROSECUTED' crossed out and 'RAPED' daubed in its place with more of the yellow paint. 'RIP BONE' but no mention of me.

The police came to see me in hospital asking questions about the plants in the attic. I denied it all. Told them it was Logan Bone's business. That I had no idea what was going on. I was in bits. Blurred bits. Off my tits on grief. I didn't care and neither did they. Just routine questions. They asked me how I met Logan Bone. How long we'd lived in the house together. Whether we were friends. Whether we were lovers. They asked me how I'd ended up in Hull. How I'd ended up on *The Cowley* and what happened the morning before my shift.

So I told them what I could. What living with Logan Bone was like. The comings and goings. The boys and the noise. I told them about my mother and father and my grandmother and God and how I'd struggled. That I'd worked all over the country picking fruit and living wild. And I told them about the bottle in the washing machine and how I'd found Logan Bone soaked in piss the night before. How I'd left him alone that morning - angry, drunk and bored. A bomb waiting to go off.

It was how we were, I said. We bounced off each other like atoms.

All the while studying their smooth cleanly-shaved faces as I painted a detailed picture of how we live down here. They'd seen it all before. Dead junkies and abandoned children. Bodies in freezers. Dads fucking daughters. Killing wives. Wives killing violent alcoholic husbands. Putrefied OAP corpses left for weeks, chewed on by starving cats and eager rats.

So they smiled and closed their notebooks and apologised for putting me through it all again. Sorry for my loss. Platitudes. They seemed happy for Logan to take his guilt to the grave to save on paperwork. Case closed.

Pity and envy. Pity from their side knowing my suffering was only just beginning. Envy from mine, that they got to go back to their kids and roast dinners and bottled beer and symmetry.

Before they left they asked if I wanted my stuff from the house. I said no. It was junk. I was starting again. A new life needed new socks and pants.

*

Pink. White. Blue. Six pills in the morning and six at night. Anti-psychotics and mood-stabilizers. Sleepers and dream-creepers. Whatever they were; Whatever they did, they worked. Curing and quietening. Pain and symptoms gone.

Now I'm on my own, fending branch and bramble. Sweating it out. Back to the old Royal. The sick Royal. The fragile Royal. I have no core strength. No muscle memory or co-ordination. Just a determination to get away. No more hospitals. No more Bernie or Helen. No more safety. Let it be. let it run its course. Survival of the fittest.

Muddied, bloodied, urgent gait. Desperation. Panic. Sudden movements. You can spot it a mile off. Haste and fear like a crackhead. A different orbit.

I'm close now. I can smell the sweet batter. The faintest note on the air, but it's there. The closer I get the more danger I'm in. Who knows what happened after I was taken away. As word spread through the portacabin pub with its barbed wire and dry hanging baskets. As rumours circulated like fag smoke and lies became truth by consensus. I could be wanted for all they know. I could have gone to prison for the weed.

All I want is the car. And some of Lucy's remains. That's all. No trouble. Just what's mine. Then I'll be gone and the further I go the less they'll care, and the longer I'm gone the less they'll remember. Until I turn up dead and they start asking questions about failures in the system and red flags.

*

It's where I left it. What's left of it. Windows smashed. Attacked with bats and scaffold poles and jumped on like a trampoline, caving the roof into a downward peak. A wing missing and all the bumpers stripped.

There's a small moraine of debris sculpted by passing cars and street sweepers and wind and rain. Leaves and twigs and fag butts and basalt. A used johnny on the back seat, dried to a crisp. 'Perv' and 'Paedo' sprayed down each side with luminous yellow paint. But no one's had the wheels.

I think about going inside. Get some clothes. I've worn the fleece since the fire. Clean underwear. There was some on the dryer, I'm sure of it. My blue jumper. Some trousers. But I'm only here for her. I don't have time for anything else.

Lucy's ashes lie in the scruffy front yard with its uneven camber down to the pavement. As I left her. Just a patch of black earth. Scant remains scavenged by vultures. I collapse back into the coarse ash, like the day she burned, bathing in her, rubbing her into my face and neck and into my mouth and tongue and around my gums.

The smell of old fires. Sulphur and charcoal. Swallowing the grit and dirt. Swallowing her. It was all my fault. But she's in me now. Her DNA and mine. In my guts and bowels. Together forever and never to part.

There's no mark where Logan Bone burned. No shape. Just a few damp matches. He's there. In the earth. But I'm not here for him. God rest his soul.

I scrape as much of her as I can into a polystyrene cup, patting her down like a sandcastle until full and heavy before carrying her back to the car, wedging her in the glove compartment. Wet ash and soil and a couple of screws.

The familiar give of the seats and yelp of the driver's door hinges as it slams shut. Seals gone, metal on metal. The dry-wretch of a starter motor and little else. People now. Women and children standing at their doors. Dressing gowns and flammable onesies. Making calls. The return of Fat Royal. Out of nowhere. Back from the dead. On the loose. Phoning the men.

Something's happening. Movement in my peripheral vision as encrypted messages ping on ancient smartphones. *He's back, he's back, he's back.*

"Oi you fucking paedo cunt!", shouts a fat kid on a shit mountain bike as I release the handbrake and we roll down the hill, and I briefly imagine an ugly mob surrounding the car, pulling me out and bricking me to death as they turn it over and set it ablaze as a warning to others. Hacking at my corpse with hatchets and kitchen knives and ice-picks, screaming *The Cowley looks after its own! Don't fuck with The Cowley!*

*

We punch a tunnel through the turbulent motorway air as the radio transmits a loud medium-wave engine note like a long wet fart, rising and falling with each touch on the throttle.

I talk to Lucy through my thoughts. An apology for not saving her. For not protecting her. For leaving her to him that day. For not seeing what was about to happen. For not obeying my instinct to remain when I knew she was in danger. He'd threatened as much, hadn't he?

I was always going back. They couldn't take me away and expect me to keep walking. She was my life. She was life. The reason I was there. The reason I stayed. My entire existence. What was I supposed to do? No goodbye. No moment. It was always there, lurking. An iron left on. Something unfinished no matter how much dope they put inside me.

I was always going to go back for her. Albeit bits, in a crumpled coffee cup. Something. A fragment. I couldn't just leave her in the yard abandoned to the soil, even if it was the first place they'd look.

Now her ashes sit jammed upright in the glove compartment as *The Cowley* disappears in the one remaining unbroken mirror, taped to the cracked windscreen as we continue in our straight line south, stopping only to eat and piss and buy fuel with what's left from my last couple of shifts at Reids. Free of any real attachment.

Full circle now. A homecoming of sorts. Where it all started. And another shithole provincial town to add to the list, book-ending the whole sorry adventure. Always running away. Always coming home to die. Just taking the scenic route. Simpler this time. No family. No fuss. No cry for help. No pity. Just a clear desire to be dead.

My years spiralling from one failed lustful love affair to the another will end as they started. Alone, naked and unloved in a strange room.

Alexandra, Penny, Sarah, Elizabeth, Nicola, Victoria, Kerry and finally Lucy.

Furniture. A bridge. A pier. A burnt-out skip, an abandoned bumper car, a fridge and a brief yet painful fling with a cement mixer.

Seven. Seven broken hearts. There won't be an eighth. It's not easy loving things. It's hard work. And it almost always ends in cold silence and terrifying aloneness.

Throw me in the sea. Burn me. Feed my heart to the fucking pigs. I don't care. It was all for nothing. I'm done. Love doesn't exist and neither does happiness. It's an illusion. A myth. Keeps the wheels turning but what is it really? Just misery and regret.

*

Pressure between my eyes. Face hot and red. Brain spasms. Pin-pricks on clammy skin as the drugs wear off. The pinks and blues and whites.

I need water and sugar but there's no time. Keep moving. Keep running. Racing whoever or whatever's chasing me. Whoever's watching me. They want me alive. To live and recover. To wear clean clothes and eat vegetables sprayed with their chemicals.

They want everyone the same. Hetero robots on the wedding trail. Even though everyone knows the wedding industry funds chemical weapons and genetic engineering. Each and every venue syphoning off money and sending it directly to Daesh and the Russians.

All part of the control. They want folk docile and malleable. Give them lager and iPhones and the Premier League and they won't cause trouble. Give them kids and a mortgage and they'll be too tired to revolt.

Religion failed. Now what? Take the legacy and spray apathy on the broccoli. Don't tell me that's not how it works. No one force feeds me market gardened defeat without paying a heavy price.

They're above me. I can see them. Lights in the sky through this filthy shattered screen. Watching from spaceships and satellites.

Their planets and misty dark towers. Cameras poking through worn carpets and rust holes. Hidden in the dashboard. Hidden in my head.

Who knows what they did to me as I slept. Logan was one of them. Watching through microscopic cameras floating in the air, clinging to dust like magnets. Protons and electrons. There's a laboratory somewhere shrinking cameras to the size of cells. Microphones recording thoughts.

Their smug complicit faces. Knowing I know what they know. The game's up. He would have been promoted, Logan or whatever his real name is. A highly trained undercover agent living a triple-life. The lynchpin in their audacious experiment. So obvious now.

That night outside Wetherspoon's. Tracking me all the way from Llanelli. Logan Bone, fully briefed and dispatched. Sat in the back of a fake builder's van, saying goodbye to his wife and kids on a satellite phone before embarking on the mission of a lifetime. Losing five stone, growing his hair out, learning to hate.

He was too badly burnt by the time I arrived. A team of make-up artists hiding round the back of the house as I entered the close. Bored of waiting. Trying not to laugh. The paramedic who helped me into the back of the ambulance. Scripted and rehearsed. The detectives at the hospital. All paid actors. Weeks in rehearsal for their moment. The estate slags and scumbag boyfriends and dirty kids. The girls in the chippy calling ahead as I left the shop. The Greeks? Fuck, not the Greeks...

So I need to die before they come for me. Because they are coming for me. Think of something else. Throw them off. *How much are the cucumbers, sir? Can you direct me to the post office? My favourite colour is yellow. Do you have a book on British Birds I can send to my uncle for his birthday?*

I'm sick, and they know I'm sick because they control the dose. In the milk. On my Weetabix. In the tea and coffee. I trusted you Bernie. I trusted your kind eyes and your grey woollen ties.

Withdrawing. Craving. Seeing stars. Hair and clothes soaked through. Things crawling up and down my legs. They want me to turn the car round and drive back in this agony. Begging to be let in. Crouched like a baby. Banging on the front door as they watch it all on CCTV until someone gives an order. Then waking me with a cup of tea and a smile somewhere safer and darker and cleaner. Deeper inside the sanctum.

It's all part of the masterplan. Well fuck you Bernie, I won't be controlled by you. If you want me, come and get me because I won't be here for long. I'm out. Dead. Gone.

Drugs and war. That's what all this is about. Big Pharma and Weapons. You want to take over the world? Fight me for it. Why else would you not just let us die? This is not a compassionate society. It's expensive keeping people alive. There's not enough for the living. You can't run humanity at a loss for the sake of ethics. So why bother with us? Why? Tell me. Explain it to me. Why keep a roomful of economically redundant fuck-ups alive when there's nothing in it for you or anyone else?

Shall I explain it to you? Lab rats. All of us. And you know it. Before your little global landgrab. Well I'm way ahead of you.

*

Black fields yield to monster car dealerships and drive-thrus as the carriageways narrow and slow, snarled up by traffic lights and pedestrian bridges.

Those four hours of wind in my face masking the burn in my cheeks and forehead. Four hours gripping the wheel hypnotised by the single wavering engine note as I confessed my sins and begged forgiveness from the cup of ashes in the glovebox.

They could take me at any moment. Roll me to the side of the road and call for recovery. By which time I'd have disappeared, passing through various departments and delivered back to Swan House with mysterious fractures and haematomas.

The orange petrol light flickers on and off. The needle flat on E. There's a burning smell and an ominous rattle. I glimpse the pier, stretching out into the deep black estuary all dressed up and nowhere to go. A Wimpy. Some pubs. The boom and bass from cars and nightclubs.

And row upon row of arcade games and fruit machines. Grabbers, punchbags and air hockey. Guns and cars. All competing for some kind of sonic supremacy beneath the spiralling disco lights and glitterballs of *Las Vegas, Sunspot* and *Happydrome.* All massively over-promising. Playing to empty houses. Just kids and fat pissheads smoking outside empty pubs, oblivious to the barren Kentish hinterland across the black, haunted estuary.

But there's beauty again. I can see it and feel it. Beauty in form and light as the machines chatter away, all eyes on me as I cruise by. Calling out. I want to stop and talk. Feel their edges and rub against them, but I can't. It's too late for that. Those days are over.

And just like that, as the din and glitter fade to darkness and silence, the Volvo dies in a cloud of oily brown steam, and we roll to a halt behind a hardcore skip in the middle of a three-car space.

Delivering me from evil, bearings lost. Uncharted territory. This is where we stop. The universe said so. I'm not continuing alone. What happens from here happens. I'm tired and I need to sleep so I'm handing over control.

I climb into the back of the Volvo and burrow down into the rubbish and the security of the footwells until completely hidden. If I could disappear I would, but this will do. I feel safe down here in the dark. Part of the earth, as sleep finally comes.

*

Dawn, and I'm shaken from my hot blur of fever and delirium by raised voices. Polish or Lithuanian. Hard angular anxious words. Coughing, snorting and spitting. It's freezing cold. The heatwave is over. Sinking into some nightmarish Narnia. Swallowed by the backseats like big brown lips concealing tongue and teeth. But I'm too big and too old and too real.

Across the road, men barge and jostle for position at the driver's door of a white transit van, like puppies trying to suckle. I can smell them. Stale and ripe. Sweat and booze and tobacco left to ferment and stew. Baggy saggy tracksuit bottoms, work boots and hoodies.

An ugly crag-faced male emerges from the guesthouse in red shorts, blue sweatshirt and yellow flip-flops.

Back at the van the fat bald driver gets out puffing on a thin panatela cigar, bowling through the crowd like it's not there.

"Morning Perky!", says the ugly crag-faced male, a fake smile in his voice. A drinker. Thin and gangly. Unshaven and pockmarked. The stink of cigar smoke masking everything else.

"What we got then?", says Perky, deep Scouse. The puppies go where Perky goes, fat with milk and work. He steps back and bats them away with his forearm. "Fuck off!"

"Okay, okay, give the man some space!", says the ugly crag-faced male ushering Perky away as the foreigners fawn and beg, hands together in prayer like he's some giver of light.

Perky points at six men from the fifteen-or-so stood on the pavement, and whatever loyalty or fraternity exists between them disappears as they're split by the prospect of pay.

"You, you, you, you, you and you..."

He picks the youngest and strongest, patting them coldly on the back like cattle at market. The rest turn around and light cigarettes, heads down. Cursing Perky. Not again. Not the fucking younger, fitter, stronger ones again. Perching on garden walls to smoke.

Yet one doesn't turn around. One hangs back. Leather jacket, black trousers and old tan loafers. Short and round like a barrel. Not dressed for site work. Not dressed for anything. But not walking away. Staring at the floor in a trance. Like he wants to leave but can't.

Because something won't let him. He's been here too many times and can't do it anymore. Then remembers there's nothing else. And it's this impasse which renders him motionless. A defeated man who came here for something better and never found it. Rendered immobile by the utter hopelessness of not getting picked by Perky.

Another 24-hours, then how many more after that? And what about after that? How will they eat? How will they ever get out of here? Even the work he doesn't have isn't enough? It has to change.

He grabs Perky by the shoulders, spinning him round, screaming and spitting in his face.

"I must work!" Stabbing at his own chest with red swollen fingers before the chilling realisation that it's finished, he's done, fucked - and he sinks to his knees, clawing hopelessly at Perky's fat hands.

It's not work he wants now but forgiveness. Then mercy.

"Get that cunt away from me!", shouts Perky as the ugly crag-faced male pulls the man onto his feet and pushes him away.

"I'm sorry! I'm sorry! Please! I'm sorry! I just need work for my family!", he begs, shoulders hunched in submission and remorse.

"Fucking sort it out Clive, or I'll go somewhere else. I fucking mean it!", shouts Perky, deep-breathing, shifting his weight from one foot to the next like a bad boxer. "Dirty foreign cunt!"

"Chill out. How long have we been doing this?", says Clive, cupping Perky's fat face with his thin veiny hands. Red chipped painted fingernails. "Pretend it didn't happen. I'll sort it. I promise."

Perky heaves his bulk into the van, the angry redness fading from his big fat cheeks.

"I'll be back Monday. Got a couple of sites in Romford that need bodies. Not that cunt though."

He starts the van and revs the engine, pulling away then slamming on the brakes, sending the men tumbling against the sides and floor.

"Never gets old!", Clive shouts on the half-turn as the rusty white transit skips second gear and disappears around the next corner.

Manis is smoking, remonstrating in a language Clive doesn't understand. Not once has he ever asked any of the men where they're from or why they're here. He stares at Manis – the raconteur, the loser, the victim – with cold stone hate as Manis shrugs his round shoulders and kicks at the wall with his vinyl slip-ons.

Humiliation. Pecking order. Clive plays it back. How many times has he told them?

You stand there and you shut the fuck up. Not a peep. Life's a bitch. It owes you nothing. Less than nothing. Not down here at the bottom of the fucking well. And not if you're some fucking refugee in a country that doesn't want you. You don't get to fucking talk. You don't get to complain. You don't have the right.

Clive runs up behind Manis. No words, just violence. A sickening crack of fist on skull. The immigrant's legs buckle, his palms and knees hitting the pavement. The others scatter, distancing themselves. He tries to pull himself up but Clive's straddling him. Punching and punching. The back of his head and ears. Clive's gold rings shredding brow and cheek as a steady torrent of blood pitter-patters on the dirty ground like rain from a blocked overflow. Let that be a warning to you. To all of you.

There's a yelp from an upstairs window as Manis's wife watches her husband roll bleeding into the gutter. And as if suddenly reminded, Clive climbs the steps emerging a minute later with the woman and a small boy, seven or eight-years-old, kicking their bags and belongings down the steps and into the street.

The boy is quiet, watching his father crawling covered in blood and dirt. A moment he'll never forget. Like all the others in his short life.

"Now get the fuck out!", screams Clive.

"Please sir!", the wife pleads in her best English, hands and fingers together in prayer, jet black hair. "No home!", she says sinking to her knees.

Clive kicks her to the floor and points down the road as she struggles to her feet, the boy left to pick up their belongings strewn like rubbish across the yard.

Why don't you react, kid? Why don't you fight? Your father stripped of his dignity right in front of you. And there you are, just picking up the bits. So unentitled.

Strange that my priority's to un-exist when everyone else is so hellbent on prolonging these unbearable lives. A desire to be happy and content and comfortable. What a weakness. Crave misery and you'll never be disappointed.

Manis climbs to his feet, grit and dirt stuck to his face as blood pours off his chin, soaking his clothes.

The other men light more cigarettes and whisper among themselves careful not to react. Sideways glances and shuffling feet. Helpless. They know savagery. They know self-preservation. Not one of them goes to his aid. No heroes.

"You wanna go too?", Clive screams at them rubbing his purple swollen knuckles, picking at the broken bloodied skin. He has a devastating power and a presence. Calm and unruffled. A savagery learnt through experience. Giving and receiving.

Hands thrust deep into the pockets of his baggy shorts, he flip-flops back inside as the men drift away up the street to buy illegal vodka and knock-off fags.

A swinging sign outside reads Hotel Ophelia in black letters and a card in the window says 'Rooms £20 p/n'. Felt-tip on fluorescent orange card, sellotaped to the glass.

I sink lower still into my bed of rubbish. The universe brought me here. I relinquished control and followed a star. And as I ready myself to leave the shitheap for the last time my hand finds something cold and damp.

The parcel of chips from two months before. The sluts in the chip shop. Their cheap perfume and wet lips. Minty fresh. The smell of burning, My cheeks tingle and flood, salivating at the thought of a meal despite the mould and rind. This is the place.

*

A bell rattles above the door.

Inside there's full frosted panes with bevelled edges, brushed carelessly with thick cream gloss. Stiff beige nets on vinyl sliders throughout and a large dusty Aspidistra lurking in one corner. An ancient red fire extinguisher in another. Leaky and rusting.

The floor's a flattened floral pattern carpet covered in clear plastic matting. Floor to ceiling nicotine-yellow woodchip paper above and below a white dado.

The reception desk stands like a pulpit, on it a half-empty leaflet dispenser and a well-thumbed A4 hardback book thick with notes and receipts and paperclips and staples. And just off the small reception a TV flickers in a smoke-filled room. Breakfast television. Applause. Laughter. Colour.

Clive appears rubbing blood and skin from his hands with a flannel.

"Can I help you?" he asks, chipper for a man who'd just beaten a someone half to death and consigned his family to unimaginable horror.

"I need a room", I say.

He stares at me, massaging his knuckles. "You're in luck."

*

Bleach and incense. Wallpaper and paint. The same thick gloss on everything - skirting boards, doorframes and balustrades. Drips and dribbles immortalised like fossils on the 1970's woodwork.

Up two flights. Movement and muffled frightened voices – men to women, mothers to children – floating down each corridor, from behind each door. Four per floor. Three floors making twelve rooms, and on each landing a tiny communal toilet and shower.

I need to be behind a locked door. I want control. Fully paid up for a few short hours. I'm desperate. Breathing hard, we climb the stairs to the second landing. The only sound between us.

A door slams overhead, footsteps on the stairs, and a woman pushes past us. Daytime emptiness. Dyed dirty-blonde hair scraped back in a ponytail and her arms wrapped defensively around her as she makes her way down with quick clipped steps. Trainers and jeans and a thick quilted coat that's too big for her. Clive smiles. "Morning Samantha", he says but she doesn't answer, already gone.

"Miserable bitch", he mutters as we stop outside room 21 and tugs his keys out of his pocket on a chain like a prison guard.

It's small. A single bed, wardrobe, night-stand, lamp and a sink in the corner. Brown carpet and curtains, a dry brown apple core on the floor by the bed and a full ashtray on the windowsill.

"No smoking. No cooking. No visitors. And no pissing in the fucking sink."

He hands me the key then pulls it away.

"Money...?"

I give him the screwed-up notes. It's all I have bar a handful of change. But I don't need money where I'm going.

"Enjoy your stay", he says with a smile and walks back down the hall.

I place the crushed cup containing Lucy's ashes on the window sill and stand in the middle of the room. Everything's old. Everything's broken. This is where it ends. When exactly, I don't know. And I haven't figured out how. But I know I won't be jumping.

*

Sam sits at the back of the hall, wrapped in her quilted coat that's too big for her as twenty or so people sit in silence listening to Kathy's well-worn share.

"I owe everything to these rooms. 'cause I was fucked, mate. Didn't give a shit about nuffink', you know what I mean? Lost my kids. Nearly fuckin' died. Eleven litres them doctors drained out of my guts. I was fuckin' yellow, mate. My liver nearly fuckin' burst. I was that fuckin' close. But I survived, and I'm here. Nine fuckin' years and countin'."

There's a smattering of weak applause and lots of nodding as Kathy sits back down. Clown. They all are. Celebrating sobriety like it's of some kind of universal significance. Even though no one's watching and no one cares. Confessions in the dark. She doesn't know why she comes. She has nothing in common with any of them. No investment in their plight or their stories. It's just something to do.

Sam's not listening. Instead she checks her phone as David brings things to a close while irritable thin women in brightly-coloured Lycra gather impatiently at the door clutching foam mats.

"Thank you Kathy. Always great to hear you share", he says glancing at the plastic clock. "Let's do a quick prayer because we're running over a bit."

Sam's eyes remain open, muttering odd words as she looks around the room at her addiction brothers and sisters.

"God grant me the serenity to accept the things I cannot change, Courage to change the things I can and wisdom to know the difference... Amen."

"Amen", she whispers as the hum of relieved chatter and rustle of anoraks slowly fills the hall. "Thank you everyone. Great meeting. Can you please put all the chairs away and take your rubbish with you. We've had complaints", shouts David over the chatter as Sam drags her chair one-handed to the edge of the room.

She senses him behind her.

"Haven't seen you much recently", he says.

She turns to face him.

"I've been busy."

"It's important you come. It's the foundation stone of your sobriety, Is everything okay?"

"I'm fine. Thanks", she says staring at the dirty scratched red and white vinyl floor tiles.

"Are you coming to Costa?"

"No, I need to get back."

"Back for what? Come on."

"I can't", she says.

There's so much she wants to say to him. The love and the hate. Instead she says nothing.

A fluorescent yoga teacher interrupts as if Sam's not there. All nipples and tattoos. High on spiritual enlightenment and body confidence.

"David, I don't want to be a pain but we only have the room for an hour.... This happens every week."

Her voice trails off into nothing as Sam walks out of the hall into the chill night air, happier in the dark and cold. Maybe he's fucking her. *Back for what?* Vicious bastard.

She sits stiffly on a damp bench behind the church and rolls a cigarette. David and his good intentions. David and his wife and kids and house and central heating and full-time job. David and his wandering cock and lambswool sweaters.

The hall empties as the addicts go back to their lives in clouds of cigarette and vape smoke. Engines. Headlights. Lifts shared. Down to Costa for late night lattes and more dull recovery tales. *Yeah, yeah, we get it.* Then central heating and TV. Insomnia. Depression. Empty without their drug but so much better off. So much happier. All that destruction replaced with growth and repair. Which is why they gather in groups behind closed doors and drink Maxwell House out of polystyrene cups to remind themselves the monster isn't dead.

Time has drawn on their faces. Scars and creases and wrinkles. Missing teeth. Faces once gaunt and purple with the sickness, now fat and pale with carbohydrates and sleep. Its fear of excitement that drives them here. But in the moment - in the drunken timeless grip of whatever it was that controlled them while the rest of the world slept and worked - it was the time of their fucking lives.

Sam stares into the darkness inhaling and exhaling, watching the smoke drift away, wishing she could go with it. Breathe herself out and fly away over the estuary. She tells herself she feels nothing yet feels everything. And hurrying away, carefully rebuilds and reinforces the walls and buttresses. Past the pubs, down the frightened streets back to the hotel, as a cold wind forces her deeper into her jacket and thoughts.

Jody's birthday. The housing application. Clive. Her meetings with Janet. Blocking out the crushing reality of what she's going through. It's easier that way. Otherwise she'd give up. And if she gave up it would be over for her. Back to the shadows. Back to the carparks and alleyways. Back to the beginning.

David was a fantasy. Dreams of normality and vacuum cleaner bags and colour schemes and recipes. His fresh smell and smooth face. His gushing naivety and willingness to help. But that was all bullshit. He just wanted someone to break. Someone more broken than him.

She winces as she walks. Fuck. Idiot. She says it out loud, such is her shame. He just wanted to take and inflict. And he chose her. And she fell for it. Fell for what she'd always fallen for. The patter. The flattery. The broken wing she could mend, when she had two of her own. And the cunt has the nerve to tell her what's good for her.

'... It's vital for your recovery. Come and have a fucking latte. You always used to...'

Fuck off...

Until you smashed my heart across the pavement. All that shit about feelings you couldn't ignore and listening to your inner voice. 'When we're together the darkness disappears'. Bullshit. I trusted you. I told you everything. Feeding the beast. The struggle. The heartache. That just gave you a fucking hard-on. That was your drug. Then the worst bit of all, you brought Jody into it. Said you'd look after us both. Make a home. Because a love like ours couldn't be ignored. Until you took a room at the Holiday Inn Express overlooking the fucking bins, and you changed, and you made me do things I didn't want to do. Told me it wasn't anything I hadn't done before.

How the fuck do you know what I've done before? Why does your little fantasy of what I may or may not be – have or have not done – give you the right to take that from me? Anyway, I didn't tell you it all. If I'd told you it all your little acorn cock would have exploded. Because you have no idea what I've done, can do, could do again.

"Sam!"

Someone yanks her arm as the words rampage through her thoughts. Anger fueling anger.

"Sam? Are you okay?"

She looks up into Donna Mackay's fat face as the hurt and hate ebbs back to where it came, like an enzyme secreted by a tiny gland seldom used.

"Are you okay Sam?", asks Donna MacKay. Sam blinks back at her.

She looks terrible. Hasn't even had any kids. Maybe she can't and eats instead. To take the pain away. Eats and drinks and giggles and smothers herself in perfume and fake tan and goes to quiz nights with sexless friends and eats doner meat and cheese from polystyrene boxes. Dotes on nieces and nephews. Pretends it's enough saying things like 'I love kids, but couldn't eat a whole one'.

Even though she looks like she could - and probably has.

"You scared the shit out of me!!", she screams, snorting like a pissed pig. Her strange little gap-teeth; the underbite. Just like at school. Never got them fixed. All painted chins and fucking glitter. Her neck a different colour to her face.

"Do you want to come in for a drink?"

"Some other time. I need to get back. Mum's got Jody", she lies. She doesn't know why.

"You got her back! That's amay-zin'!", shrieks Donna Mackay. "I was thinking of you Sam, I really was. Maybe we could get together for a coffee or something. I'll text you, yeah?"

"Do that."

"Where you livin' now? Still round here?"

Sam doesn't reply, just looks down at fat Donna MacKay's painfully-red toes poking out of her market stall wedges.

"So good to see ya, Sam, yeah… Is it good to see me? Look at us! All grown up!"

"I better get back", says Sam, starting to hate her all over again.

"You get back to her *girl*!", then "Love you Sam!" But Sam's already in the shadows, back into the darkness and the alleyway towards the inglorious parade of bedsits and B&B's. Beautiful old four storey houses sliced and diced and left to rot, a stone's throw from the bright lights and candyfloss.

She lights another cigarette and imagines she's somewhere else. Following the smoke high into the air above the old river, Jody hanging onto her back as they laugh and giggle and look down at the fields and villages and shops. Just the two of them, tumbling into the sky. Higher and higher until the earth becomes curved and they stop breathing because they don't need to.

There's a quickness in her step, like a child but much quieter. Determined to make it up the stairs and through the door unnoticed. The reception clock says 8.50pm. Jody will be asleep.

She wants to hear her husky sleep-voice. Feel her floppy heat, eyes barely open. She wants to phone John and ask him to wake her but that would be wrong. *Play the long game*, Janet always says. *Be the best version of yourself.* No sudden movements. They'll think something's up. Sit in your room. Cry. Miss her all you like but don't phone John. Phone Janet, but don't phone John. That's what Janet's there for. That's what Janet said.

She pushes higher, each corridor lit acid green by a single wall light.

The new guy in room 21 startles her, staggering out of the bathroom soaked in sweat and white as a candle. A bottle of bleach thuds against the floor as she pushes past him up the stairs. Fucking junkies everywhere. Junkies and creeps and fucking rapists.

Inside her room she sits on the floor and texts Janet. *'Feeling shit. Saw David. Wanted to phone Jody but didn't'* then deletes it.
Janet doesn't need to hear this. Validation, that's all it is. Same as those pricks at the meeting.

She should never have gone. But why should she stay away and risk everything she's worked so hard to build? The trust and respect. Gone in a moment. A moment of weakness.

Yes she wanted to see him. She wanted to see him because she loved him. And she wanted to feel it again. That painful longing for someone who's so close yet so far away.

She could text him now. Tell him it was nice to see him. That she wished she'd gone to Costa. Let him think she's willing to forgive. Go back to the Holiday Inn Express and let him do that stuff to her.

Tell him she likes it. That she liked it all along. Then message his wife for her own good. Because she deserves to know, and he deserves to be found out.

Why shouldn't he know how it feels to lose everything?

She scrolls to his number. *'David AA'*. She can hear Janet yelling at her not to. *You'll lose her for good!*

The phone slides out of her hand and she wants to text Janet and tell her she let the phone slide out of her hand instead of texting David to lure him into some fucked up revenge trap. Instead she turns off the light and chain smokes two cigarettes as she looks out over the silent street completely unseen.

IV.

Devastating hot and cold sweats and nausea. Everything tinged a strange greenish yellow.

I don't know how much I was taking. Whatever it was they were giving me. I didn't think about that as I fled Swan House through the woods. I didn't think to ask them for a repeat prescription or a magic bag full of pills.

Which explains the ominous painful pressure behind my ears and an ache in my shoulders. Specks and spots and imaginary voices. Brain twitches and anxiety. Sweats. This is withdrawal but there's no Librium here so I have to front it out. Make peace with it. Take the pain. Welcome it in. Remember it's not forever. It's leaving. Whatever it is, it's leaving. With every breath and droplet of perspiration. Shit and piss.

But my chemistry is shot. I just want to sleep and drink water as my body and mind scream out for more, alone in this small dank room.

I remember her now. The girl on the stairs. Same one as earlier. Her face gurning and melting into a fat one-eyed surgeon in a leather apron surrounded by tigers, blocking the light as he drills into my skull looking for the tumours. Abandoning his precision instruments to gouge at my exposed brain with his bare fingers.

Now medieval embalmers sew me up with black needles and coarse thread. Exposed organs and cavities. Applying oils and lotions to my dead grey skin as robbers rifle through my pockets for a chainwatch and purse, before dumping my body in the freezing Victorian mud - a pearl-handled knife in my guts.

Dreams, past lives and visions.

I don't care about anything else. I can't. My human brain is too small. Too slow. So I slide into this hot vibrating delirium and explore these new worlds.

The car's fucked. The money's run out. Energy and fight, all gone. It's what the universe decided and the universe knows best. If I turn back now they've won. I'll die as I was born. Screaming and naked, wrapped in a sheet.

Pain doesn't scare me. It's all I know. I just wish I'd been able to turn it into something. Some mould theirs into fire and set the world alight. Use it as fuel. But I was always on the backfoot, lacking that extra yard of pace. I've always let my pain hold me back and hold me down, and this is no different.

Another wave of sweat and sickness shakes me in its jaws. Say a prayer or something. Dry mouth, on my knees guzzling from the small sink in the corner with its untidy mastic edges. Spiders everywhere, watching me. Thousands of them. Eyes in the dark. Googly spider eyes blinking and disappearing off into hell. Assuming hell is down. No one really knows. Maybe it's up.

Reminds me of a kids' show but I can't remember the name. Aliens or monsters or something like that. From the 80's.

And suddenly the room is all around me.
Everywhere I look. Everything I touch, smell, feel. Smaller and bigger, living and breathing. Vertical-striped wallpaper. Unfinished carpentry. Skirting boards flecked with tea, blood or shit.

The carpet and rug full of bits no vacuum cleaner could ever pick up, and the bare lightbulb hanging from the ceiling, dead-centre. Its plastic housing baked yellow at the base, split and warped by bulb after bulb after bulb.

It's thrilling.

I take the bleach with its stubborn cap and childish pink bottle, and retreat to the corner of the bed like a monkey with a doll. Protecting it in my fat clumsy cradle. As if the room might take it away or talk me out of it.

Cap off. The twitch and sting. Clean. Sparse. Uncontaminated. Kills all known germs, dead. Destroying the bad and protecting the good. Killing evil. Dirty microbes. They're just the start. But they grow and they multiply and they spread. Climbing and conquering, exploring then dominating until it's too late. That's why you have to kill them at source. When they're young, because once they have numbers you're fucked.

I raise it quickly to my lips, the bottle. Ready to drink and die. But not really. Not now. Something's happening. Something big. A tremor, verging on joy.

Then – I see her watching me.

Revealing herself.

Her dark silhouette, bathed in orange lamplight bleeding into black like fur.

A rush of chemical euphoria as my arms go limp and warm and I turn giddy, hiding my face in my hands, peeping through my fingers at this magnificent imperfect shape on the wall. That fat wonky black heart.

Hello, you...

Lowering my hands so as not to startle or frighten her back to wherever she came from. This is real. Not a dream or an hallucination. I can see it, the orange light shining through the window, the crushed cup of ashes casting her shadow. I'm clean and cured. No more shudder and sweat. No more fear.

She's talking now. Says it's okay. That I don't need to die because I have so much to live for. Saving me from the poison. That point before the point of no return. Shining a streetlight through a window behind the crushed cup, projecting a black heart onto the wall of a room in a hotel I broke down outside in a car now dead, with exactly enough for one night.

Providence.

I was brought here. To feel this. Lucy wasn't the prize after all. She was a conduit. A martyr. It was only ever this room. Sat here for a hundred years. Built just for me. Our trajectories pointed at each other like love lasers. Lucy died to set me free, like fucking Jesus. Logan Bone the executioner, nailing her to her cross.

I climb off the bed and kneel in the shadows as the bleach bottle slides onto the floor.

"What's your name? Tell me your name", I whisper, leaning my forehead against the wallpaper in the middle of the great dark heart.

Ophelia, she says.

"Of course."

Breathing hard against her with my mouth wide and lips flat and cold, kissing with just my tongue, licking her layered grime and nicotine.

She laughs nervously. Dry, old and neglected. Embarrassed. Now it's her turn to be shy as the heart flickers momentarily crashing us into loveless darkness. But it's only a moment. A reminder of the old life.

"It's okay. Don't worry", I whisper.

My thoughts are clear and smooth like oil. I'm a man. I feel suddenly loved and muscular and warm. The man I always wanted to be. A love like no other. Hotel Ophelia, a monument to that. Holding us in its womb, birthing us up here on the second floor.

She smiles and I comfort her. All of me, as hard as I can. My head spinning with desire for her walls and carpets and ceiling. Her air and space. Her sink and pipes and paint and mites and dirt and dust.

The drugs are gone. I'm back.

*

Clive sits at a vanity mirror in his basement applying foundation to his raw acne-scarred scarred face, humming as he pouts and licks his teeth. Liners and pencils and gloss. On the table a bottle of supermarket gin, its top smeared red with high-end lipstick.

A floral cotton sarong over pink silk panties, and suspenders above perfect white stockings. Matching bra drawn tight across his flat chest, supporting nothing. Hairs sticking through. Ridiculous yet serene. Ugly yet feminine. Moving in a slow rhythm as he goes about his routine, swigging in time. All part of the dance.

There was nothing he wouldn't do. Boys. Girls. Young. Old. The mermaids that haunted the estuary, choked up on plastic and opiates.

He'd grown bored of what was expected. He did what he wanted. Kept things shallow and simple. His sick perversions and callous nature no longer a mystery. He was what he was. A thief. A liar. A bully. A killer. Feared by the weak and scared of the strong, he sought only to satisfy his wayward appetites and inflict misery.

And the hotel afforded him that. The frightened and desperate. He brought them in. He shipped them out. And everyone who passed through earned their keep one way or another.

Confronted with the ultimate horror of human capability, his eyes glazed and his heart yawned and his brain sighed. Men and women. Runaways. The lost. Some eaten by Coco. The others boiled and buried. Dissolved and flushed into the sewers. Trapped in fatbergs or dumped far out to sea. Coco was a psycho. How long could it go on? He'd been to prison and wasn't going back, swimming out of London and washing up on a beach where he found Ophelia and regarded his new surroundings greedily.

The dressing room table is tidy and warm. A scented candle burns off the lazy hanging smoke from the cigarette hanging off his lip. Billie Holiday and fags and perfume, like a 50's boudoir. Red bulbs, powder and dust. The heartbeat and buzz. The rattle and shake of the snake.

He takes a wig from a safe in the floor - a copper bob – and places it on his flaky powdered scalp, adjusting it in the mirror and licking her lips, as she hums her approval. Coco rises slowly to her feet and closes her smoky eyes, swaying to the music as she runs her fingers down the front of the pink silk knickers. Watching and touching, admiring her work.

..Moonlight and Love Songs never out of date; Hearts full of passion, jealousy and hate; Woman needs man and man must have his mate... sings Billie.

Beyond a painted rattan three-part screen is an unmade bed. Tracksuit trousers and hoodies. Dirty socks slung over a chair. Wine bottles and ashtrays. Sour, damp and cold like men are. But she's not a man, as she takes another mouthful of gin and taps out a line of the good cocaine. Throwing her head back triumphantly as areas of her broken brain spark and fizz with total self.

Three minutes to ten o'clock.

The downstairs CCTV screen plays a rotation of storyless scenes from lounge, landings and corridors. All is calm, all is dark. And it's under this darkness that Coco is released. Walking the streets unknown and unseen. Kept in the safe with the money and drugs until Clive lets her out.

*

Sam's not frightened. It's been going on too long.

Playing the long game. Keeping her head down. Holding her breath since they took her girl away. Jody deserved better than being left in cars and damp flats with strangers or worse. But she needed help. Weren't they supposed to put her back together? Not just take the child and show her the door. All they did was send Janet. What fucking use was that?

Janet didn't get it. How could she? Just another fat bored empty-nester looking to ease some middle-class guilt. That's unfair. Janet was the only person who'd shown her that much attention without wanting to fuck her. And she gave her money. A few quid here and there. Which was against the rules.

9.59pm.

The shadow under the door, then the push and the squeak of the sticky hinge. You're early.

Coco's drunk, her white painted face glowing ghoulishly like a lantern. The usual cocktail of booze, tobacco and perfume. Grunting and panting, stopping to catch her breath. Sam draws the sheets around her in some last-ditch defence as Coco drops the robe and sinks to her knees, crawling across the floor like a creature ready to pounce.

Long limbs and big hands and feet like a wolf; the one dressed as grandmother with her frilly quilted nightdress and cap. Cock and balls spilling out of the tiny tight panties. Chest hair and ribs. Spots and dots. Pus-filled.

Sam pulls back the sheet revealing the thick black dildo and wriggles down the bed to receive her, legs wide apart. It's a familiar play. No script, just a rough storyline.

"Did you get my letters?", whispers Coco.

"Clive must have kept them", says Sam.

"Why would he do that?"

"Because he loves me and he's scared."

"Scared of what?"

"Love."

Coco pulls Sam towards her and kisses her on the mouth – burning her with stubble, smearing her with lipstick - then grabs her by the neck and slaps her hard across the cheek. It's the usual. Hard and angry. Coco's hands wrapped firmly around Sam's throat, restricting airflow. But It's over quickly as Coco starts to moan and loosen her grip, rolling off the bed onto the floor.

She crouches on her hands and knees as Sam edges across the bed and kneels down behind her, parts her buttocks and ruefully inserts the dildo.

Focusing hard on the white stickers on the black soles of Coco's size-12 stilettos as she gasps and sobs. '£29.99' crossed out and '20' scribbled in rushed red biro.

Clive took Sam in. He gave her shelter and sanctuary. She looks at Coco's blotchy tear-streaked face. The vulnerability no-one sees. And she feels warmth and pity. Which is why she plays his game, fucking him once a week with a sixteen-inch black rubber strap-on. It's the least she could do.

Coco moans and shudders, pushing back and giving forwards, in and out, faster and easier as her muscles relax and stretch. The bit Sam likes. She always was a thrill-seeker. Always wanted something new and different. A sparkling young optimist who slipped and fell in her rush to escape.

RIP the sparkling young optimist.

Goodnight Coco. Sleep well.

*

You make me feel warm and dry and clean. No cold or pain. No dirt or filth. I'm free from all that. Free from my earthly body of fat, bone and flesh. No psoriasis. No purple swollen ankles and sore tendons. No tooth decay or ingrowing hairs or fungal growth and thick milky toenails. No whiteheads or blackheads. No IBS. Nothing smells or weeps or oozes or bleeds.

I'm wrapped in a cloud, weightless and ageless. I feel full and empty. I have no future or past. Everything is you and me. As we hang lazily in the air looking down like smoke.

Is it death? It feels like death. Or how I imagine death to be. And if it is, then I don't want to live. If this is death then give me death. But if this is life, show me the way. Take me with you. Just this part. Not the rest.

I'm a cartoon character, drawn on paper with sharp lines and perfect proportions. Muscles and long blonde hair. He-Man or Hercules. You're perfect you. And I know it can't be real. I'm not a cartoon. And nor are you a woman, in body. And you're talking to me now, telling me it'll all be okay. And I'm crying in your arms. My cartoon arms and legs and hair and clothes. Fitting you. Tears of relief. Not sex. This is not physical. It's metaphysical. Tunnels. Fires. Caves.

You and I running from the air to the centre of the earth. From Logan Bone. From Skeletor. But we're not frightened. We're just happy. And we're not running, we're flying. Because we're smoke, remember. A big brilliant cloud of smoke.

*

I lay where I fell. The room's as I left it. The bed clothes rucked where I fled to the corner, scared of the thing I didn't know. Naked and smiling, staring at the angle of the wardrobe, each wallpaper stripe. The window frame and radiator, and a small recess that serves no purpose. In love.

I want to know everything about her. I want to spend eternity endlessly repeating her name. How it feels in my mouth and on my lips. Finger and probe. Examine each surface. Each layer of paper and paint. The textures and relief. Each crack and stray thread and hair. Each dead tick and mite. Each skinflake. To create a map. Multiple maps. Multiple dimensions. Smells and tastes. The composition of its dust and dirt. Send them to the lab for analysis. Scanned for prints and DNA. Everyone who's ever been through that door and why. What they saw. What they said. What they felt.

There's a white patch the shape of Denmark where the bleach spilled out.

Panic.

I was meant to be dead. But I can't be dead. I have to be alive, for her. But I can't afford to be alive.

I didn't budget for survival. It can't happen. It wasn't part of the plan. They'll find me and take me back. Shit. But It's too late for regrets and rational thought. Things have changed. I need to clean. To be clean. I need money. I need perfection. I need to stay. All of those things. Whatever it takes. I need to be here to set up our home, our bed. I need clothes and soap and cologne. I need control.

I need to wash and dress. I need food and water. And I need it all before dark and her return. When the lights come on and she leaps from the shadows.

There must be factories around here. Processing plants. Apple pies and ice-cream and chips and Yorkshire puddings. Rhubarb lattice. They must take people on. They must need good reliable Englishmen. Cash in hand, no questions asked. The foreigners turn up drunk and raise suspicion. There must be work for good hardworking men like me in a town like this.

Trust the universe. The universe brought you here. Saved you. God with a big G. Working through serendipity and coincidence. Believe in its power to swallow you whole and spit you back out on the doorstep of this hotel. Delivering you from evil. To Ophelia, through shape and light.

Unless the Universe is working for them. On a kick-back from the grand conspiracy and its shady agents, hiding behind the big curtain. Maybe they paid the universe. Maybe they are it.

I guzzle water from the sink, struggling to get my mouth round the tiny angled faucet. I need to flush out the germs. Start over. Clean and serene. Piss the colour of lemon juice not lifejackets. She can't see me like this. But money first. Buy another day. Remain. Think. Plan. Talk. Fuck. Love. Ophelia.

*

I'm stiff from the woods. Lactic acid in shrunken muscles and fat limbs. I don't know where I am or where I'm going. What's left of the Volvo juts from the curb like an aftermath. Like it's been stolen, crashed and dumped. Everything but torched. *Pervert* still clearly visible down one side. *Paedo* on the other. I head the way I came, back to the sea.

Mental state. Disorientation. Time. Physical condition. All the variables. I have nine quid in change. The wind's ten times stronger on the seafront, blasting needles of sea-rain into my face. The estuary waters smashing like glass.

Streets strewn with litter, lettuce, shit and puke as the wind whips leaves and polystyrene cartons into their familiar dance, resting in corners as seagulls surf thermals, dive-bombing chip wrappers and bins. All to the beat of empty cans and bottles tumbling along the pavement.

An old man with a long grey beard sits in a hospital wheelchair, one leg wrapped in clingfilm swigging from a blue bottle of white cider. His pin-striped suit trousers ripped at the crotch exposing his balls and a wild white bush of grey matted pubic hair. He doesn't care. He's barely there.

Everything's closed and padlocked. Each shop-front obscured by hostile security shuttering. *Ye Olde Chippy. The Wimpy. The Kursaal. The Foresters. The Mitre.* All shuttered and deserted. The arcade bulbs, dark reds and greens, wiring visible behind the lifeless lights. No fairy dust. No magic sheen or veneer. Even the toilets are padlocked.

A chalkboard breaks its tether and falls violently to the ground with a slap-bang outside a tiny archway café. It reads 'Full English £3.50'.

Inside a man in a white paper hat fries bacon on a hotplate he tends with a scraper. Spanish or Mexican by the look of him. Iranian maybe. Bursting at the seams of his dirty white apron.

A waitress delivers two £3.50 fry-ups to a pair of matching builders in high-vis jackets, heavy on beans and tomatoes and cheap white toast.

"Yes my friend?", he says scraping the hotplate.

"I'm looking for work", I say.

He smiles sympathetically. "Wrong time of year, my friend. Come back in the Summer."

"I've worked with food", I say but no one's listening.

The high-vis builders side-eying me, their sweaty pink heads bobbing and ducking as their hangovers slowly leave them. Smirks and bass murmurs. The waitress's mocking smile.

The weakness in asking. The humiliation of refusal. The indignity of unemployment. Because everyone has to pay their way. That's the working class way. You can do what you like as long as you're working. As long as you're in on time.

I step back into the wind, no closer. A little further away maybe. There's nothing beyond the pier. Just a crap fairy grotto and some waxworks, so I double back with the wind behind me, blowing me back past the arcades to a row of pubs, catching the eye of the waitress once more as I go.

*

Red velveteen upholstery and red-and-white floral carpets fill the space. Red-topped stools line up along the bar. White carnations on the red window sills. Gleaming brass footrails and kick plates.

"We're closed! Come back at eleven!", comes a voice above the sound of a vacuum cleaner.

"I'm looking for work", I shout.

The machine dies and she steps into view holding a plastic utility tray full of *Mr Sheen*, old toothbrushes and yellow cloths. Earlobes drooping under the weight of ugly gold earrings, her face a mass of kitten-soft wrinkles dusted with face powder.

"Just so you know, you're on the cameras. Now, what did you say you wanted?"

"I'm looking for work", I repeat, feeling suddenly sick.

"You'll be lucky", she laughs. "Wrong time of year, see. Come back in May when it starts to pick up."

My cheeks pool with saliva and she grows distant, drifting up and away as my legs give way and I fall backwards onto the carpet, aware only of the cold brass rail waiting to be buffed and polished.

*

I drift back in. I don't know how long I was out. She's still talking, stopping only to suck on a cigarette that she rests in a blue ashtray. There's brandy on the table in chipped mugs.

"...It's all them fuckin' immigrants, see. Used to be able to take your pick, but not no more. 'cause they all work for fuck all, see. All they eat is potatoes and cheese slices. You go up there...", she says, waggling a finger in the air, up and behind her, '...and you'll see what I mean. Like rats they are. Disgustin' it is. Terrible what this town's become. Used to be beautiful. Everyone came here. Posh people from London, you name it, but not now. It's a fuckin' shithole now. Fuckin' disgraceful. People come here now, think they can do what they like. They have fuckin' Polish shops! Special shops for Polish people with all Polish food with everything in fuckin' Polish. I tell you what, I wouldn't want to bring up my kids round here. Not now... Are you feeling better, love? Had a bit of a turn didn't ya..."

I rest my head against the wall, craving cold. A tiled floor or a window pane.

"...of course, that's the other 'fing. Everyone's off their fuckin' heads on god-knows-what-else. Robbin' the place blind. Last year a girl cooked her baby. Thought it was a fuckin' chicken. Roasted it alive. Poor little fucker. She was foreign an' all."

She pauses briefly to smoke and sip her brandy.

"Where you stayin', love? You got somewhere nice?"

I open my mouth to speak but not enough comes out. Just a single phlegmy syllable that catches at the back of my throat. She leans in smiling.

"Say again, love? I'm a bit deaf."

"Hotel Ophelia", I say.

She tenses. Becomes cold. Her expression one of horror.

"They should knock that shithole down for a start. I wouldn't let my dog shit in there. Any of them places. You hear all sorts up there. Little kiddies gettin'... wotsit... you know. You need to be careful. Get out while you can."

She drains her mug. "Well, I'd better get on. If I hear of anyfing' I'll let you know. If you're still around that is. In the area, like."

She watches me leave, making sure.

I vomit on the pavement, back out into the wind and rain. Strings of saliva and snot flying off my chin and beard as I crouch on the wet slabs. A smell of brandy. A girl on her phone, pushing a pram, smoking a fag. Tracksuit. Gold hooped earrings.

"What you looking at?", she spits, lips tight across her teeth. Marching up towards the pier and the hill up to the high street. Fourteen, maybe fifteen. Maybe thirteen. A child.

"… just some fuckin' tramp on the seafront", she shouts spitefully into the phone as the hungry seagulls gather, spying a meal, and the old boy in the doorway with his cock out laughs and waves.

Welcome to the club, son.

*

Janet pulls up outside the hotel in her small silver Audi, oblivious to the radio waffle. DJ Banter and local ads for garden centres and wedding fairs. Half-thoughts drift around her head. Things she hasn't done. Things she needs to do. Things she'll never do.

Pop in and see her dad. Take him a loaf and a couple of bottles of something and invite him for Sunday lunch. Talk about the racing and the weather and his lungs.

She needs to get back to Eileen about the whole Tuscany farmhouse thing. Mike thinks the pool's too small. Will it be hot enough in June? What's the chef situation? Could the prep be done elsewhere so the kitchen's not out of bounds for three hours a day? Mike sends her things as he thinks of them. Sometimes just words with no context. She doesn't reply. It's dictation. She just turns them into lists.

He gets cross if she doesn't.

Mike's out tonight with Credit Suisse so doesn't need dinner. Maybe a snack for when he gets in. A sandwich or something. Just in case. Even though she tells him he shouldn't eat after 10pm. It's bad for his digestion Makes him snore and fart in his sleep. And it could give him cancer, even though he says that's hogwash.

He likes the word hogwash. It's so dismissive and final. As if nothing she ever says or does has any real value. Unless it's servicing him. Food. Clothes. Holidays. Diary. Dry Cleaning. She's his project manager and he's the project.

Brexit's a noise in the background. It won't affect her. Mike retires next year. He says market uncertainty plays into his hands which is why he voted Leave. There's profit in crisis. He only ever thinks about himself. He doesn't care if people get sent home, or if industry relocates and whole communities are destroyed. All he cares about is money and that stupid bike.

She has some money put by just in case. About twenty thousand, should she ever need to get away and start again. He'd fight her, she knows that. Men like Mike don't like to lose. Pride. Greed. He'd try and destroy her and he'd probably succeed. She left once, when the boys were small. Went to her mum and dad's. He begged her back. Said things would be different. And they were for a while, but it soon returned to normal.

Sometimes she thinks about where she could be and how she could feel, but gets distracted. She's too old. It's not sex she wants. That ship's sailed. And the awkwardness of a companion? Some stuffy old man who likes walking holidays and Sudoku. *Bleurgh!*

Mike still excited her. His drive and control. Zero patience. Focus. And when he was nice it took her back and she felt happy. The rest of the time they kept out of each other's way. Her mastectomy changed things. She became less in his eyes.

Like when they lost the baby before Andrew was born. He didn't want to know. It was like she'd never existed. But she did exist because Janet gave birth to her, wrapped her in a towel and took her to hospital in a carrier bag while Mike was at work. Her tiny dead daughter, sat on the passenger seat of a Peugeot 205 as she bled into a bath towel and avoided potholes.

The passenger door opens with a pop and Sam slides in next to her shattering Janet's calm. Fresh fag-stink and chewing gum and negativity. Holding a present in a carrier bag, the black and gold wrapping paper crinkled and cracked like she wrapped it days ago and cradled it ever since.

"Hey, how are you?", asks Janet, patting Sam's knee.

Sam ignores the question. "Sorry I'm late."

"You're not."

She's wearing that scarf. The same purple and yellow patches on her neck. Fingers and thumbs by the looks of it.

"How's your week been?", asks Janet looking for a tell.

"Went to a meeting last night."

"What's happened to your neck?"

"Nothing."

They wait for the lie to settle and fade.

"Anything you want to talk about?"

"No."

*

They drive in silence, the whole short conversation replaying in their heads. Two versions.

"I can't believe she's five already", Janet says.

"Time flies", says Sam. She's embarrassed and ashamed. Last night is still right there. Coco's hands round her throat. The smell. Her cries and moans. Retreating like a wounded beast, back to the sewers as the townsfolk slept soundly in their beds.

Janet reverse parks across John and Mary's driveway.

It doesn't matter for the visit. They need to be in the house by law.

The bruises. They never talk about them and Janet never writes them up. She should, but doesn't. She doesn't feel it's her place to. What good would it do?

Meep, meep, meep goes the parking-assist.

If she doesn't want to talk about it that's up to her. She's entitled to a sex life. That's not grounds for anything official. Who though? Who gets to lie with her and undress her, playfully tugging at her underwear, pulling them down over her buttocks. Feeling her pale soft skin against theirs. Playing with her nipples and tasting the wetness between her legs.

Who fucks her? Their hands clamped over her mouth and around her neck, grabbing at her thighs, pulling her on top. Who is it? What's his name? Does he live there? She's never been in. Never seen inside. She just imagines the rooms and smell and lives piled up on top of one another.

Mike wants her to stop. Sometimes she does too. But why should Mike tell her what to do? He says she gets too invested. But what does he know? He's never there, and when he is he doesn't listen. Dismisses it. Belittles it. Social work? What kind of a stupid job is that? There's no money in people. The sick and the suffering cost us billions, he says. Billions that could be spent on infrastructure and tech.

He earns the real money, not the pocket change. Banking and LIBOR and the markets. The important stuff. She doesn't even know what it looks like, or what he does there.

There must be coffee shops and pubs he uses that he thinks nothing of, yet she never sees. Dealing floors and back offices. Faces on the train. Half his life, his alone.

But Sam can do what she likes as long as she tests negative and goes to meetings. There are plenty of scumbags who neglect their kids. Starve them and leave them unattended, yet keep them and show no attempt to change.

Abusive partners. Trips to A&E. Kids, innit. Always getting into scrapes. Climbing trees and skinning knees. Breaking their arms for no apparent reason. Concussions in their sleep, falling out of bed. As these *wankers* – she shouldn't think that word and hates herself for it - happily skip through loopholes denying all knowledge.

A cycle of addiction, prison and abuse. Products of the same. Maybe Mike's right. But she couldn't do it if she didn't care.

Sam wants to change. She's taken responsibility. Too much. Thinks she deserves the shit and the suffering and the bruises, wherever and whoever they're from. Punishment for what she did. But there's something in how she talks about the hotel that frightens Janet. It has a hold on her. Like she can't be without it. The comfort of the cage perhaps. She switches the engine off.

"Come on then."

Crazy paving and white-painted cinderblock walls and rockeries. Converted bungalows in brown and beige. Cats dozing beneath cars and vans, and the feint smell of creosote. It's all so quiet. Just birdsong and the hum of a distant main road.

Seabass. She said she'd do Seabass on Sunday. Mike likes Seabass.

*

Janet settles on the sofa, perched on a cushion with Sam's file open on her knees. A green dog-eared folder full of forms and stapled printed sheets. NHS and Essex County Council. Photocopies mainly. A dismal life-story told in A4 and tick-boxes.

She's just there to observe, make sure it all runs smoothly and report back if it doesn't. The house is pretty simple. Clean and neat. Toys piled up in one corner of the small lounge. A framed 'Keep Calm and Follow Jesus' poster over the red-brick fireplace housing the wood-burner and a small pile of split logs and newspapers.

It's small. There's nowhere to go. No flow. No escape routes or privacy apart from the toilet and the shed. Her and Mike couldn't live there. Especially when the boys were back. Can you imagine?

John is small too. By-the-book and earnest, dressed in baggy jeans, red Crocs and a loose-fitting T-shirt. Forty-eight nearly forty-nine with short grey hair beneath a blue beanie. There are pictures on the wall in oval wooden frames of a boy in his dark blue uniform. Of all three of them. Janet knows about the boy. When he was born. When he died. She knows everything about the Franklins. Mary's Citalopram prescription. How much she drinks. John's redundancy. It's all in the file.

Sam sits nervously on a beige recliner, wrapped in the big black coat, staring at her battered shell-toe sneakers.

"Can I get you a tea or coffee, Sam?", John asks, not waiting for an answer. "Janet? Tea?"

'Tea, no sugar, for me", she says looking over at Sam, fighting the urge to answer for her like a mother might. "Sam, John's talking to you."

It comes out wrong. Like a dressing down. Sam looks up from her feet, at Janet, then John.

"No Ta."

Always the same. Curt and rude. Barely looking up.

"Jody won't be a minute. She's putting her birthday dress on upstairs. She wanted to look her best for you. She's very excited." He disappears into the kitchen. Sam stares at Janet, still wiggling her toes, arms folded.

"Please try", Janet says just loud enough for Sam to hear. "Why don't you take your coat off?"

"'cause I don't fucking want to", she says with a teenage scowl.

Little feet overhead. On the stairs. In the hall. Then Mary enters with Jody behind her, gripping Mary's fingers and leaning into her legs as she coaxes the shy child out.

"Hello Sam", says Mary, thin and sinewy like a climber. Boyfriend jeans and clogs. Hair scraped back. No make-up. Relaxed. Almost mumsy for her age. Sam smiles, brimming with hate.

A better mum to Jody than Sam could ever be. Because she left her on her own. Abandoned her in the middle of the night, in a cold damp flat with no electricity. Spotted by a passing motorist. Caught in the headlights, screaming for her mother who was scoring gear nearby. Injecting in a windowless room surrounded by junkies and needles and foil and shitty sofas, while police drove her baby to the station wrapped in an anorak.

"Come on Jody. Look, it's mummy", says Mary with Christian glee.

"Jody, it's mummy! Come on! Come and cuddle mummy. I've come to sing you happy birthday. Look, I've got you a present", says Sam.

It's a bribe, tempting her back towards the womb. Jody walks cautiously looking back every couple of steps. Sam drops to her knees, eyes wet with tears, and wraps the little girl in her arms.

"We'll just be in the kitchen. Shout if you need anything", says John but Sam doesn't hear. Trying not to cry. Trying not to pick her up and run out the door with her. Trying not to fall apart. If Janet wasn't there they'd be gone.

Both hands clamped around her head, studying her perfect face and form, then pulling her in tight, for fear someone might rip her away. She can smell the newness of the pink princess dress. Feel it's cheapness.

Janet sips her tea as pots and pans bang in a sink somewhere out back. Too much milk.

"It's alright, baby. It's mummy. Have you missed mummy? Jody, have you missed mummy?" Jody looks confused. "I love your dress and your hair. Did Mary do that for you? Did you say thank-you? Mummy's here Baby, and mummy loves you very much."

*

Janet looks around the tatty café. It's a long time since she's been in a place like this. Years. She normally makes sandwiches or goes to Leon. Fresh ingredients, reliably and ethically sourced.

There are ten or so red-topped tables bolted to the floor, strewn with sugar and salt and mismatched condiments. Squirty plastic tomatoes, sticky to the touch. The front door propped ajar with a 6kg purple kettle-bell to disperse the clouds of wet grease rising from the fryer.

Mugs of weak tea arrive, bags in. No saucers or side-plates or serviettes. A weird lamby aftertaste. She's not drinking that.

"Have you thought any more about college?", Janet asks, trying not to push.

"Haven't had time."

"You need to show them you're taking your future seriously."

"I am, by not fuckin' using."

"It's not enough."

"How am I supposed to concentrate on some poxy college course?"

"It would send the right message that's all."

"Why are you giving me shit?"

"I'm trying to help you."
"I don't need fuckin' help."

"No? I think you do. I think you need a lot of help."

"Every other fucker gets a flat."

"You had a flat and you lost it."

"So you think a child's better off without her mother?"

"Depends."

"Fuck you."

"Look, I wouldn't be here if I didn't have faith in you." They sit in difficult silence as the waitress brings the toasted tuna melts and fries. "How are you doing for money?"

"Getting by."

Janet fumbles in her bag and slides two £20 notes across the table.

"What's this?"

"Just take it."

Sam claws it into a tube and stuffs it in her pocket. It feels like a deal.

"Thanks."

"Be a grown up. Take responsibility. Play the game with John and Mary. Things will get a lot easier a lot quicker."

Sam looks back at her food, head cocked, prodding a chip into a glob of ketchup.

"Did you get anything in the post this morning?", Janet asks.
"I haven't checked. Why?"

"They've brought your review forward."

"What does that mean?"

"It means they could make a decision in the next couple of weeks."

"Am I getting her back?"

"It's a step forward."

"When will you know?"

"The hearing's on the 12th."

"What do you think?"

"There's a chance. But please - *please* - don't get your hopes up. Nothing's guaranteed."

Sam hugs Janet across the table as weak tea slops across the formica top. Janet liked seeing her happy. Unaware of her own delicate beauty.

Her soft perfect skin. Her sad pale blue eyes. Her constant frown and crooked teeth keeping the secret. She often imagined Sam the teenager, in a short skirt and cardigan and black bra. Blue ink spots on her shirt. Flirting her way through life.

Smoking weed at lunchtimes. Meeting men in cars. Real men. Men with jobs. Not the schoolboys who went home and spunked on their bellies.

But men who smelt of oil and beer and tobacco. Hard dry hands. Dirty fingernails. Picking her up at lunchtimes in their cars and vans, taking her back different.

She'd considered taking her in herself but she'd have to resign and Mike would never agree to it. And even if he did there'd be problems down the line. He'd want her. It was asking for trouble. But waking up in a house with Sam and Jody was something she often thought about.

The house was empty without the boys. And Mike was hardly ever there. She was lonely, and there was something about Sam that made her feel a bit more alive. Even if that broke the golden rule, Janet didn't care. And she didn't think much of Mary and John and their charismatic Christian schtick either. People aren't perfect. And she was no different.

V.

I turn away from the seafront and the wind. Up the hill past the tattoo parlours and mid-range chain hotels with impressive views of the dead estuary. Up to the wide-open toothless mouth of the high street and the tatty rat-run of charity emporiums and pound shops and bookies. An all-you-can-eat Thai buffet. A Greggs. Phone repairs. Butchers selling cheap cuts and trays of dirty eggs.

People with bits missing. Teeth and ears and fingers. Alkies and addicts forced into the rain on their restless quest. Old men with tartan shoppers, and parrots and pythons. And fat old women on mobility scooters with massive tits and ankles trailing slow sons and scruffy dogs. All framed by the spray and rain.

Soaked through I scour the pavement for dropped coins. The quicker I get paid the quicker I get back to my love and the more time I have to prepare my next move.

Rest. Love. Fuck. Sleep. Go again.

I need a process. Dry clothes and toiletries and places for cheap healthy food. Lose weight, gain strength, feel well. A barber. A razor. Neighbours who can help me when I'm sick. A community built on trust and virtue. Then we can grow. Heal this wound and create a society where all are welcome, regardless of colour or affliction, and raise our families with acceptance and tolerance.

I'll sell the watch. It starts today with the Omega De Ville.

The Omega people, I'll call it. We'll start again. A brand new civilisation dedicated to goodness and love. Away from this. Somewhere else. A new world. Free of ugliness and pain. Just me and my people. It's an epiphany and it quickens my step. A goal beyond the daily toil. An endgame.

Kodak memories flood back in full saturated colour. Printed on thick photographic paper. Vinyl-coated and finely textured. Rounded corners. Memories of cinemas and jewelers and tiny independent shops like caves, stacking stay-press and *Slim-Jims* and Gabicci. Pierre Cardin, Farah and Lyle & Scott. Chaotic churches of casual fashions. The stuff of dreams for pubescent boys as they stir from childhood slumber into the full glare of sub-adulthood and all its mis-sold promises.

Sunny summer Saturday mornings. Something for the house or a new pair of Nikes. A Hi-Fi stack system with Dolby sound. A dishwasher. A video recorder. New-fangled and futuristic. Walking into Dixons like they're about to make contact. Then queuing excitedly in McDonald's for giant Big Macs in polystyrene boxes.

None of this CFC bullshit or single-use plastic. Pure consumption, then straight to landfill. Fuck that amateur-night Thousand-Year Reich shit. This stuff will last an eternity. Unrottable. Like the fighting spirit of this new consumer class. Swamp-dwellers climbing out of the docks covered in shit and London Clay, growing legs and lungs then slithering to the provinces for a taste for America.

The pawn shop's still there. Stubborn. Resisting the slow glacial creep of corporate retail. Metal grills poised above its windows like portcullises. Toughened glass and CCTV icons. Not accusing but warning. A faded Alsatian window sticker barking the words 'I LIVE HERE'.

Inside, a glass counter-top cabinet full of rings and lockets and watches, each one embedded in faux velvet cushioned trays, trailing tiny hand-written tags on strings with descriptors and price. An electric fire pumps out gassy wet heat from the back workshop where things are fixed and valued. I can smell toast. Slipping the watch off my wrist the stink of dirty wet clothes fills the air. The white-faced Omega with gold hands and Roman numerals. My father's.

The old man shuffles out from the back, crumbs around his mouth. Brown slacks, brown cardigan, brown woollen tie. A pair of frameless varifocals perched on a bulbous blue nose. The texture and lustre of orange peel. Suspicious watery red-rimmed eyes.

"Can I help you?", he asks, like I have no business here, the bread stuck to the roof of his mouth and in his teeth. I offer him the watch and he hesitates, gesturing for me to place it on the counter. He slips on a pair of latex gloves and turns the watch over, angling his head and swallowing hard.

"Who's HW?"

"My father", I say.

His eyes dart from my sodden hair to the pool of rainwater at my feet. Old trainers with burst stitching. Tracksuit bottoms and purple fleece.

"Can I see some ID?"

"I don't have any", I say.

"No ID?"

"No."

He shakes his head and licks his teeth, probing for crumbs. "I don't buy off junkies."

"I'm not a junkie", I say pulling up my sleeves.

He stares at my arms then back at me. Calculations. Intuition. Gut.

"Get out of my shop", he says. "Or I'll call the police."

"It's not stolen", I say again. "It's all I have left."

"Then keep it", he says. "I don't want it."

*

Cash Converters sits at the business end of the high street, the window full of junk and glare. Games consuls and weight-benches. Hulking great electric organs and exercise bikes draped and coiled in silver tinsel and fluorescent orange starbursts. A grotto of desperation and debt.

A fat twenty-something stands behind a glass cabinet the whole length of the store. Pony-tail. Acne. Three-stone overweight. Watching me as I browse a cabinet of darts accessories – flights and shafts - checking I'm not stealing. Shoving things down my pants or up my sleeves.

"You need help?", he calls across the shop, just me and him, his face reflected in a dozen mirrors.

I put the watch down on a small plastic tray on the glass top. His name badge reads 'Marc' with a 'c'. Fake-snake boots. Combat trousers and a red regulation cotton shirt polo short. Slurping weak tea from a company mug.

He takes an eye-glass and inspects every last millimetre of the face and housing, squinting at the winder and bezel.

"I might have to get the manager in on this one", he says, spinning on his block-heels and shoving his face into mine. "...which is me, because he's on jury service which makes me acting manager till Saturday. You look fucked mate. Don't worry, I won't tell anyone. Business is business. So what are you on? Meth? Smack?"

"I'm not on anything", I say.

"Sure", he says winking and tapping his nose. "Ask me no questions I'll tell you no lies. Same in this business, mate. Don't you worry. Your secret's safe with me. It's all about the moolah." He rubs his fingers together and holds the watch up into the light. "Okay, let's see if we can get to a place that works for both parties. Good condition. Couple of scratches on the glass. Nice movement. It's engraved so needs a new back. The watch market's an unpredictable beast. But I've got a good feeling about this one."

He taps his temple and closes his eyes, taking a moment. "Okay, fella. Here's the deal. You could take it down the market but you'll probably get SHOT bruv 'cause it's like fucking Compton down there, blud, serious..."

He points an imaginary gun at me and pulls the trigger.

"Soooooo...twenty quid. Best I can do."

"It's worth five times that", I say.

"Not to me, it ain't. And not to anyone else around here. If you want to go on the interwebs and wait a month, that's up to you, Geez. But if you want hard cash. Right here, right now, I'm all ears."

"Thirty."

"Twenty-five. Take it or leave it", he says, his index finger hovering over the till release. "Shall I prepare the paperwork, *compadre*?"

*

The beach is deserted. Just litter and seaweed and thousands of cockle shells pumped out from the sheds after processing and dumped by the tide.

Out in the shipping lane colossal container ships edge slowly across the horizon as the chimneys on the Isle of Grain belch clouds of something. Smoke or steam or chemicals. A combination of all three. Is it a power station? It's too big to be a factory. Huge jutting pipes like superguns pointed at hostile alien forces.

A few hundred yards offshore windsurfers reach hard, back and forth, their jagged sails pulled perpendicular to the wind, like the dorsal fins of some monster fish with teeth the size of feet.

Up and down they go. Glad to be alive. Glad to be free. Glad to be monsters.

Back at the hotel my car's being winched onto the back of a white pick-up.

"That's my car", I say.

"It's been reported", says a tall skinny man in baggy green overalls, his thumb on a big green button operating the whirring hydraulics.

"Please. It's all I have."

"Too late."

"Why?"

"Because it's on the back of my fucking truck, that's why", he says before relenting. "Look, I'm just following orders, mate. If you want to talk to someone, phone the fucking council. Or I'll take it off for fifty quid. But you won't get more than that for it down the breakers so there's no fucking point."

He reaches for a clipboard, ripping off the yellow top-sheet and shoves the pink copy into my outstretched hand.

"You've got 28-days to pay the fine or it goes to the crusher."

"What about my boots? They're in the back."

"Take 'em. Just be quick."

I'm down to a pair of work boots and some shells. Not much for a lifetime. Everything else slowly jettisoned. Clive stands on the porch smoking weed, sheltering from the rain in surf shorts and the yellow flip-flops.

"That your heap of shit is it? Had to phone it in I'm afraid. Fucking health hazard."

*

I wait in the dark, the shells laid out in a perfect heart shape on the window sill around the cup of ashes.

When she comes her black heart's bigger than before. I shudder, fighting for breath. She's all I've thought about and all I have. Ready this time. All done up. Perfumed and primped. We don't know each other, yet we know enough. It's sudden.

Kissing, licking then fucking. Awkward and polite as our teeth knock against one another and things don't go in as they should. I'm suddenly incredibly aware of myself and what I'm offering. I'm not enough. My breath. My weight. My skin. Why would someone like her want someone like me? I'm dirty. I'm sick. I'm ugly.

Maybe I should just go. Walk away. But I can't and she tells me it's okay. That I'm all she's ever wanted. So I flatten myself against her and hope. It's different to last night. There's a familiarity and a warmth. A naïve desire to be close to one another. A new awkwardness.

It's electric She's aroused to the point of collapse. Like she's about to crumble around me. Brick dust and mortar and dry rot and plaster. The pipes and basin and carpet and windows, filthy on both sides.

"I got you some pretty shells", I whisper.

I want to tell her I love her. I want to know everything about her. What hurts her. What frightens her. What makes her feel, but something stops me. Maybe I've built this up. I mean, we only did it once. Maybe it was just sex to her.

I'll ignore her. Pretend she's not here. Pretend I can't see her. Move rooms. Move out. Go back to the beach and the sea or the hospital. Admit that I can't survive out here and I can't form the kind of relationships that humans need to feel nourished. That I just want to be on my own in a room with a TV and food under the door and a steady supply of multi-coloured pills in waxed paper cups.

"I'm scared", I say, finally.

She doesn't know why. She doesn't know what's riding on this. My very existence. The rest of my life. She controls it all. She is my life now. All of it. It all belongs to her.

There's a long pause, then she tells me she loves me too. And suddenly I'm powerful. My voice is smooth and confident and no longer a stuttering apology. Deep and strong like my father's. Like HW's.

"We've all lived different lives. Does that make sense?", I say, and she tells me it does through micro-vibrations in the masonry. Through a release of her dry wallpaper scent. And her skirting board scent. And her window sill scent. And her ceiling scent. And her telegraphed thoughts and feelings.

*

I take ill in the night. A throb in my gut that comes and goes in waves. Ophelia sits at my bedside offering comfort as I slip in and out. More dreams. Basketball. Lions and Tigers. My mother and father in a rowing boat. A Victorian dinner party aboard a royal ship, the air thick with laughter and cigar smoke and the clink of champagne flutes.

A new heat. Across my forehead and chest and that debilitating agony in my stomach that just won't cease. Pulsing and pumping like a new organ. I have to be patient. Ride it out. It can't be food. I haven't eaten for two days. It has to be something else. One of the billions of possible microscopic hazards I've been exposed to in the last 48-hours. But I can't be ill. Not like this. Not laid up and unable to move. Unable to work. It's all against the clock. Planned out in chunks. I can't skip a chunk. Not now. Further down the line perhaps when I know what I'm doing and the Omega People are up and running but not now. Miss one day now and I'm fucked.

Ophelia blows cool air on my face and strokes the soles of my feet as the pain in my guts shakes me in its jaws.

*

I can see their red faces in the dark lit by fire and flares. Standing below the window of the presidential palace. Looking up at the room bathed in orange. Thousands of them. Millions maybe. As far as the eye can see. Knowing I'm here. Ailing. Dying. Their King. Waiting for a sign. As the news crews in vans with huge satellite dishes and countless generators broadcast live to the nation and helicopters hover overhead desperate for a glimpse.

In a statement released very early this morning his doctors urged for calm and an end to public hysteria and said the President's condition was stable although he would need twenty-five pounds by lunchtime to secure room 21 and the future of the Omega People. It's thought his mother and step-brothers are currently returning from America to be at his bedside...

*

In and out. Drifting. Then suddenly awake, staring at the ceiling of the tiny landing toilet, at the dead bugs in the light fittings; dead moths, mosquitoes and spiders. Blurred through frosted textured plastic. My head held fast between the cold porcelain and the wall. I don't know how I got here but the worst is over. The convulsions and sweats have stopped. Just lethargy now.

The door bumps against my feet. Once, twice. The girl from the stairs, standing above me, blocking the light. I struggle to sit up but I don't have enough. The room's too small and my legs and arms too weak.

She helps me back to my room and fills a mug of water from the tiny sink, looking around the empty room.

"Do you need an ambulance", she asks.

"No", I say.

"Don't let Clive see you like this. He'll throw you out", she says. "When was the last time you washed your clothes?"

"I've only got these", I say.

"Take them off. I'll get them washed. You stay here and rest."

No sympathy or pandering, just solutions. Maybe that's what mothers do. She doesn't even turn her back as I undress and wrap a bedsheet around my waist. She stuffs everything in a plastic bag and my thoughts drift back to Ophelia and the wedding.

*

I sleep while she's gone, and when she pushes back through the unlocked door I'm where she left me. I don't know how long it's been. An hour, maybe two. She hands me the bag, light and warm and smelling of fabric softener. Unlike the wet stinking wodge she took away. Neat folds.

"Take a shower", she says. "You'll feel better."

She looks over at the shrine of shells in the window recess. "What the fuck is that?"

"Just shells", I say.

When I get back the bed's been made and my clothes are laid out on the smoothed counterpane. Purple Fleece. Tracksuit bottoms. Dry pants and socks. My old stinking trainers upside-down on the radiator and my boots beneath the sink. A blue carrier bag at the foot of the bed.

My skin is clean and pink and smells of faintly of orange zest.

"Why are you helping me?"

"Because you need help", she says.

Five quid from the forty Janet gave her. She couldn't just leave him in the toilet. Whatever he's doing, the reason he's here. She couldn't ignore him. Fuck Clive.

The pink bottle of bleach in the corner of the room, the same one he dropped on the landing outside the bathroom. She thinks of a shit joke but stops herself. The shells, the bleach. Too many questions.

There's a carton of soup and a sliced white loaf in the blue carrier. So I eat then dress in warm clean clothes.

Look after yourself, she said. *Stay clean and dry. Keep the room tidy. Store your food. Consider every action and reaction.* If she didn't say it she meant it. Like a room should be. Like a home. Like a home should be. Whoever she is, she was sent by the universe. By Logan Bone's weed farm and Lucy's death. A guardian to the founding father of the Omega People.

Tonight I'll ask Ophelia to marry me and when – if – she does me that honour, we'll marry in a clean room. Me in my fresh dry fleece and tracksuit bottoms, her in her orange blackness. And I'll remove my clothes neatly and stack them on the floor at the bottom of the bed with my bread and soup, before we make love, then sleep.

*

Multi-coloured lights flash and dance on a loop, reflected in glitter balls and the polished metal trim of every machine. Unspectacular in the drab daylight as I wander through the red and silver aisles, scouring the patterned carpet dropped coins. There's money everywhere. Loads of it. Filling great glass cabinets. Piled up in manned change booths. In the bellies of row upon row of fruities and bandits.

A gang of kids crowd the entrance to the arcade, teasing a helpless security guard.

"You do that again, you're fucking banned!", he yells.

"It's not over the line", whines a stringy blue-faced adolescent in a shell suit edging his front tyre forward a millimetre at a time. Bored and on the wind up. The security guard can't win. They're kids. You touch a kid and you're fucked. Ban them and you have to enforce it. And these kids ain't scared of nothing. It's a game to them.

"It is over the fucking line!", he says.

"It fuckin' ain't!", shouts the kid.

"Just fuck off, all of yous!", says the guard.

"You fuck off. You can't talk to us like that!", shouts the kid.

"I'll fucking talk to you how I like. What ya' gonna do?", says the guard.

"I'll get me' dad!", shouts the kid.

"Get your fucking dad then!"

"He's fuckin' hard", says the kid. "And me' uncle's fuckin' hard an 'all. He just got out of prison."

"Good for your fucking uncle!", shouts the guard. I lean into one of the coin pushers with my hip, conscious of the CCTV signs and cameras, but nothing gives. I bump it again pretending to play, but nothing. Then I get my hands under the steel lip and jolt it a couple of centimetres. As it drops an alarm sounds and a handful of coins rattle into the tray.

"Oi!", shouts the guard, as the kids abandon their bikes for a better look. "Oi!", he shouts again, tripping and tumbling onto the hard carpet to a fanfare of triumphant laughter. I snatch the money and run, out of the arcade past the Wimpy. Then up a narrow alleyway full of bins and dogshit, barely a shoulder's width wide, to the big carpark at the back. The coins are hot and wet in my clenched fist. Thighs rubbing, lungs burning.

"Fucking stop!", he yells down the alleyway, but I'm too far ahead and the echo of his footsteps slow to nothing as I head away from the seafront towards town and the cover of the streets and more back alleys.

*

The coins beat out a march in my pocket. Not enough to live on, but it's a start. Start of a fund. A way of life. Something that'll grow and grow.

I find an abandoned supermarket trolley at the back of some lock-ups, part obscured by nettles, poking up through the wire. Why didn't I think of it before? We need transport to survive. Logistics and infrastructure. To move things from A to B, and get it to market.

Cracked taps and broken lamps. Anything metal. Records and tapes, long defunct. Bin-to-bin, dragging my reluctant trolley behind me. It's only when you look, do you see. Fuck the human race. It's exactly what's been holding me back. Expectations and standards. Norms. Consumerism and its wasteful dishonest ways. The real treasure's down here. Abandoned next to trees. Strewn across pavements. In bins and boxes ready for landfill. I'm out of the race despite this thinning human disguise.

In the distance a high-rise block looms large. A huge sandy brown monolith, yellow-clad up the middle, above pedestrianised bowl sloping down to two lifts and a piss-stinking staircase that service the eighteen floors. Four huge waste chutes depositing rubbish bags into four steel bins on wheels, wedged with chocks and surrounded by junk and clutter. More bags. An ironing board. A blood-stained mattress. A broken bedframe. Some backless kitchen units. And several small green polythene bags full of dogshit.

A bunch of kids kick a ball around the concrete parabola, the gentle slope an extra man as the ball scuffs and skids and the kids curse and tease. There's a pair of broken painter's steps but it's enough to get me up and over, and the boys watch, giggling as I climb into the giant stinking drum.

There's nothing in it. Just bags. Bags and bags. Stink and give. Soft under foot like wading through mud. Then there's movement. Whispers, footsteps, high-pitched cries as the bin starts to move and the scratchy wheels rattle and scrape over the patchwork of asphalt and concrete in the shadow of the block.

Zig-zagging one way then another as they whoop and scream, tormenting the trapped animal with rising hysteria. No way out. Like a puppy in a sack full of bricks. Let's kill him. Let's burn him. Fill it with petrol and incinerate him as his blistering hands claw at the sides unable to get purchase. The ultimate death, like a Brazen Bull.

Round and round we go, out of control, the sky spinning. Physics and fear. It feels unstable. The bin too high, the wheels too small and hard and everything moving far too fast as the whip momentum gambles with the surface and eventually – inevitably - I'm flipped hard to the ground. The kids squeal with delight, fleeing down well-trodden rat-holes and back-doubles.

My hands are cut and I'm covered in a putrid slime. All I can do is retrieve the trolley and make cover. Then keep moving. I've already lost valuable time and energy. But it's a lesson learnt. Kids are cunts. Bins are shit. Take the sure thing. The open road. Not the gamble, because the house always wins.

I'm three hours from eviction. Three hours from losing Ophelia. Which means I have three hours to make my money minus the time it takes to get back to the hotel.

*

To my left is an old long-gone second-hand car dealership with folding doors and a forecourt piled up with fridges and furniture instead of Fords and Vauxhalls.

A makeshift dustsheet sign stained with large red letters reads 'House Clearance. Cash paid £££'. Inside, brown herring-bone tiles covered in newspaper and loose lino between stacked banana boxes and tea-chests. Floor-to-ceiling steel shelving bowing under the weight of magazines and bric-a-brac. Dusty appliances, glass and china. More cheap repro furniture fills what's left.

I don't notice the man in the corner until he speaks.

"Can I help you?", he says pulling himself up on old knees.

His voice doesn't match his face. Long greasy brown-grey hair tied back in a ponytail. A boozy redness in his cheeks covered in grey whiskers. A holed argyle sweater, tracksuit bottoms and tan moccasins, Everything smells of tobacco and piss.

"I've got some stuff to sell", I say gesturing to the trolley.

He takes a pencil from behind his ear and starts to poke around prodding and poking, counting and muttering

"I'll give you a couple of quid for the monkey", he finally says.

"How much for the lot?', I ask him. He sighs. It's a play. Screwing up his nose and sucking his teeth.

"I might be able to get something for the taps." He gives out another big sigh. "I'll tell you what, I'll give you eight quid for the lot."

"I need eleven", I say. "What about the books?"

"No one reads books."

"The monitor?"

"Computer stuff dates too quick."

Eight quid leaves me short. The scale of the task. The inevitable failure. Like feeding an addiction. I can't do it. Not every day. Starting from scratch. What good can come?

"Sit down. I'll put the kettle on."

"I need to get on."

"Let's just see if it works first. Don't get many people in here these days", he says pulling up a bright blue office chair on wheels and lighting a fag from his tobacco tin. "So why are you pushing that bucket of shit around, again?"

Laughter gets caught in his throat, becoming a hacking cough. He spits a mouthful of thick grey phlegm on the floor and works it into the dust and with his foot.

"Just trying to make rent", I say.

"Where you staying?"

"Douglas Street."

He sucks his teeth again. "Bit fucking spicy up there, son."

"It's cheap", I say looking around his emporium of junk and salvage. "What happens to all this stuff?"

"Most of it goes to auction or boot fairs. Roots Hall's a good un' and it's not too far. Down by the football ground there."

As he speaks he fishes in his pockets and counts out some change, piling pound coins into a flush stack in his hand. He leans forward and jams them into my hand.

"Here you go. You get better at it as you go. I pay good money for copper as long as it's not war memorials. And bikes. People will always buy bikes. And if you get really desperate there's a recycling place on the landfill. Pays cash, but it's tough work, believe me. What's your name, son?"

"Royal", I say.

"Royal, eh? Never heard that one before. I'm Ray", he says relighting the roll-up hanging off his lip. "Be careful, Royal. Some nasty cunts about."

VI.

Another night on the Golden Mile. Fights, booze and 3-for-2's.

The Rat-a-tat-tat of copper and silver reflecting in smooth scratched parabolas to the excited shrieks of pissed-up kids escaping the inescapable. All garishly lit by strobes and bulbs, watched over by the giant plastic clowns and penguins with rolling eyes and buck teeth. The air is thick with fumes and the sounds of cars scraping over speedbumps in first gear. Drum and Bass. Doof-doof-doof as girls get fingered on Recaro seats, then driven home to Shoebury or Southchurch or Eastwood.

The trolley rattles along behind me, swinging sideways with a tinny metallic rise and fall. Then as I bend to pick up a five pence piece he's on me with all his weight, grinding my face into the pavement, spitting in my ear as the trolley slip-slides towards the kerb and the traffic. The timbre of a ride cymbal followed by a crash and blast of a horn.

"Back for more? Thieving prick!"

"It was just a few coppers!", I say.

"Thief's a fucking thief!"

Globs of saliva, cold on my neck. Blood and concrete on my lips and tongue. All I can see is the tiled slope and row upon row of blurred bandits and slots.

Voices on my blind-side. Teenage girls again. Pink saliva pools on the pavement as he jams his knee into my back. He's battling on two fronts, fending them off with one outstretched arm. I can't fight or run. I need that money. Deliver it safely to Clive so I can stay. Glad of the rest.

"What the fuck's he done to you, eh?", shrieks a girl. I can't see her face but I can imagine it. There's two of them. Angrily finishing each other's sentences like some two-headed beast.

"He's a fucking thief", he shouts, his breath a mix of tooth decay, fags and cheese & onion.

"He wasn't even in 'ere! He came along the front!"

"He was in here earlier, so mind your own fucking business!"

"He's fuckin' 'omeless!"

The guard shifts position, his anger vibrating through my back and buttocks. "Just fuck off?!"

"I beg your fuckin' pardon? You can't fuckin' talk to me like that, you cunt!", she shrieks, pissed and indignant.

"I'll talk to you how I like."

"Big man 'aintcha! Beating tramps up for no reason?! You're pafetic, mate! Pafetic!"

"I nearly died for this fucking country!" He lifts up his shirt to reveal an old scar. A bullet wound from battle. Pink and shiny.

"No one gives a shit, mate!", she screams with delightful glee. "Bet you didn't even know what you was fighting for!"

"Fuck you!"

There's something in his voice - trauma and shame - as the others laugh and his body goes limp. Just the rise and fall of his chest like he's asleep or thinking. He doesn't need this shit. It was a pointless war. It was for nothing. And now just a story and a souvenir. At least he didn't lose his legs.

"Your wife know you like showing young girls that scar, does she? Shame it's not on your cock. Or d'ya get that blown off an'all?"

"Looo-ser!", they sing. *'Loooooo-ser!"*

I buck and wiggle as his limp bulk shifts and I roll onto my back, breathing uninhibited now, as the lights flare in my watering eyes. The deep blue of the darkening sky and a taste of blood. The sound of a punchball and the ding of a bell. *Flash! Bang! Ding! Whoa!*

I'm so cold. I want to climb into the footwell of the Volvo and sleep for a year. Wake up when it's over. But even that's gone.

"It's fuckin' assault, that's what it is!", shrieks the girl. "We could get you fucking stabbed mate! Add that to your fucking scar collection!"

He taps the Go-Pro pinned to his chest. "Yeah, well this is all on camera so I'll have you nicked for making threats."

The murmur and laughter of the assembled crowd, like before when Lucy and Logan burned. It's me again. The entertainment. Tragic. Filming and posting; tagging and hashtagging. #tramp #trolley #bully #loser #TheTrolleyGuy #TheFatTrolleyGuy

"There you go mate. 'ere's your trolley, yeah. Have a good night, yeah", says the girl, pulling the trolley along with her. She gives me a quid from her purse. I can smell sugar and alcohol on her breath. Perfume.

"You need to have a word wiv' yourself mate!", she yells at the guard. "Fucking cunt."

She doesn't see his pain. She's not looking. Just waving her arms about, stabbing the air with fake fingernails. "You're a fuckin' disgrace!", she shrieks, walking off in the opposite direction as her indignation gives way to whoops of cruel laughter. The whole thing soon forgotten.

The guard struggles onto his knees. He doesn't see me watching. An unguarded moment. What he's become. A moment of introspection. Proud of his past. Proud of his job. Unable to confront his truth.

I feel remorse. He was just doing his job. I am a thief. What a loser. Me and him. All of us. Cannon fodder.

"Do you want a hand?", I ask.

"Just go", he whispers not looking up.

*

Ophelia's waiting for me when I get in.

There's something different about her. Sexier. More confident. She's inviting me. Licking her teeth. But I'll make her wait. She's never seen me look this good. Tired, dirty and bloodied. She wants to soothe my pain. Tend my wounds. Because I'm the man, going into battle so she can stay back and keep house.

She wants me there and then, admiring my shape and form. My grazed shoulders and elbows. Dirty streaks up my arms. The scratches from the bin beneath the flats as I fought for her. For us.

She can see the micro-tears in my muscles. The broken fibres around my bones and cartilage. Healing stronger. That's evolution and I'm evolving. Changing into something else. A hunter and gatherer. A husband. A father maybe. Ready to further strengthen our race through standard reproduction.

Her voice is weak and shrill from the pure thrill of knowing what I'm prepared to do to keep us together. I crouch low against the skirting board, stroking the smooth painted surfaces, tenderly kissing and licking the carpet and the boxed copper pipes that lead to the hand-basin, full and feminine. The window sill and the base of the curtains, flicking at them with my tongue.

I spread my hands and legs wide against the orange wall, moving my hips in a slow circular motion. I'm glowing. I'm a star in the sky. Both of us. Burning up and looking down. Lost in her. I start to move through the hot bricks and plaster to her pink sweet-smelling skin and genital flesh. Further than I've ever been. My toes and calves cramping. Heels knocking and rocking. A roar of pleasure as I ejaculate on the wallpaper and re-enter the physical space, back through the crumbling brickwork and the damp plaster. Standing there empty, cold and in love. That was the first time. The first proper time. The first time we felt each other. No shyness or discomfort. Shuddering with sex-joy.

"You make me feel like a real man." I whisper, my top lip still stuck to her.

She's too overwhelmed to speak, watching me from all angles. Admiring every inch of what's now hers.

"Marry me!", I whisper and she accepts in a heartbeat and we're married in that moment.

*

Clive haunts the corridors, leading men in bad suits up and down, in and out of locked rooms.

I see no one. Just voices and footsteps and high-pitched cries, day and night. Lonely frightened children. Every room a capsule of fear. Human sediment dumped by a river as it meets the sea and loses power. Like the dirty estuary we live on.

I don't care who they are or what they're feeling. I can't afford to. I crave only the sanctuary of Ophelia. To create a sustainable existence for as little as possible. I see and hear the men from my window, congregating at the front of the hotel. I smell their odour and cigarettes and hear their ringtones. Clive barking orders, and the revving of engines. And in the dark when Ophelia sleeps I watch the street and the people who pass along it. Hustlers, dealers, vandals and thieves.

My love for Ophelia was always going to cause problems with the other rooms. Jealousy. Culminating in violence perhaps. Bullying. No one likes to see others happy. I feel it in the silence and the shadows. Whispering as I walk by. The rough keyholes and cracks beneath the door. The toilet flush. The stillness of the fire extinguishers. The tacks and screws that scratch my arms and catch my sleeves on the stairs. And the banging. The banging and the voices overhead.

No one else exists. I hunt and fetch. I come and go. Return and heal. And when I'm with Ophelia nothing else matters.

It was different with Lucy. She was always there, waiting. Ophelia arrives with the night and leaves with the dawn. Makes me wait and enters like a spirit. She's a mystery. That's what she is. A mystery.

*

Dolls. Thirty maybe. Thirty-five. Identical in their crushed water-damaged pink and yellow boxes. Squashed and ripped. All called Suzy. All with identical blonde pigtails wearing identical pink sequinned mini-dresses, white frilly pop socks and black ballet pumps, staring out of the crinkled plastic windows like whores.

Painted dot-eyes. Hipless and lipless. Jointless arms and legs. Perfectly slender. She even sings. It says so on the box. 'Pull my string and hear me sing!'

...I love ye-oo! I love ye-oo! I love ye-oo!...

She loves me. They all do. In unison. Based on nothing. Just an unconditional pre-determined plastic love engineered in a Chinese factory. I don't want to hear Suzy sing. And I don't want her love. I have love. This is about logistics. I need to get them to market without delay. The market being Ray.

Dumped in a wheelie bin on an industrial estate just off the A127 two miles north of the seafront. A giant toy wholesaler with offices in Shanghai and Hong Kong. Tipping samples and duds. It came to me in my sleep. I'm a businessman now. And I need to think like a businessman. What would Branson do? Would he rifle through high-rise wheelie bins, or would he be sourcing stock straight off the line?

It's Roman thinking. Give a man a fish and he'll eat for a day, and all that shit. I'm not fucking about. I'm on the up. I won't be spread across the pavement like some two-bit mug. Fuck you. I deserve respect. Are you listening to me? I've spent too long foraging and scavenging. Accepting what's left over. Crumbs from some low-rent King's table. I deserve more. I'm a man. I'm the man. Muscles that tear. Fibres that snap and repair in my sleep with love and sex and white bread. Sleep and water.

A 1985 Bedford flat-bed pulls up in the middle of the road and a giant jumps out waving and pointing, coming straight at me. About eight-feet tall, in a burgundy workman's jacket, unbuttoned and exposing his tattooed chest. *Then -*

Crack! And I'm down. Hit across the legs with a golf club. The dogs are barking. Two Mastiffs. Frog-faced and fat like barrels, paws up on the muddy slobbery windows.

"Waddya thinkya daa'n?", he hisses through gaps in his gums as he kicks the trolley over, spilling the dolls. "Keep your facking hands to ya'sel or 'oil cut 'em off, ya thieving cont! I'll break yis' facking hands, ya cont, and 'oil snap all da fingers on 'em!"

He pulls a club hammer off the back of the truck, silencing the dogs' incessant din, and starts to smash the dolls' tiny delicate faces. Crushing heads and legs. Torsos splintered and chewed by power and violence. The tiny dresses and shoes ripped from their small bodies. Naked, broken and scattered like war dead.

Disembodied. Decapitated. Delimbed.

I love you! I love you! I love you! they sing, begging for mercy and rescue. Pleading not to be left out here to die like whores, a million miles from home. The trolley's next. Bringing his hammer down with devastating force and accuracy shearing off each wheel and buckling the mounts. Stopping only to get his breath back and check his work.

"You wanna fuck wid dees' streets, you gunna fuck wit' us, ya hear? If I sees y'again 'oil do ya fackin' bollicks!", he bellows, his giant hammer aloft like Thor.

There's nothing left of the dolls. Nothing salvageable. He gets back in the truck, leaving me in the road surrounded by pink plastic debris. My tiny empire destroyed. The slobbering dogs are barking and he slaps one across the muzzle to quieten it as they pull away. A slap then a punch. And when the truck's gone, just a ringing in my ears.

Fuck this. Fuck it all.

I need to sleep. I have a hangover from chemical fear and dehydration as the traffic whizzes past me on the dual carriageway.

For a second - maybe less - I consider the ease of walking into it, piecing together the logic and visualising the impact and aftermath. The clean-up. The traffic disruption. A fireman hosing away any trace.

I came here to die, so why not fucking die? How hard is it, when death is so much easier than life. This constant search. Walk into the traffic. Do it. Just do it. For everyone's sake. Breathe in, breath out.

O- on the inward breath, *-phelia* on outward breath. *O-phelia. O-phelia. O-phelia.* Come on. *O-phelia, O-phelia, O-phelia.* Calm down. You're doing the right thing. Love is love. You have to work at it. Fight for it. Marriage is hard. Just ask anyone.

*

There's a smell of weed on the downslope of the old river basin as it falls away back towards town.

Two voices, low, slow and smoky. Deep with THC. Two boys really, in their teens or very early twenties on a path lined by short black winter rosebushes. Both talking in murmurs through held breath as the spliff goes between them.

Me, hidden by a hedge on the corner of the street.

It's so quiet and still. The smell of creosote and fresh grass cuttings. A cat in the road. A plane in the sky. A mountain bike leant awkwardly against the wooden gate. Bright green with black handlebars. Ray said he'd take bikes. I feel so visible. Like a clumsy daytime drunk. No other movement. Just the occasional passing car.

There will be witnesses. From behind white nets, through the double glazing. Calling to their husbands as they potter around in the shed or the garage.

There's a strange man in the road.

Snippets of conversation. Something about a baby. A sister. A bloke called Peter Belt. Laughter.

A small white coarse-haired terrier sniffs at the boys' feet.

This is where they live. The class above. Functioning poverty. Complacent. Not like us, at the bottom. The desperate and forlorn. The lost and lonely. Screaming and flailing. Razor-sharp. One false move and you're in the grinder. Snagged by hair or clothes.

No, these are the small time weed dealers living with their nans and retired civil servants handing apathy down from generation to generation. Propped up by good credit ratings and long-term illness.

Quiet and comfortable, safe and warm. Away from the chaos. Where the system works.

My leg's not broken. The proper pain will come in tomorrow or the next day. Regardless, there's no escape on foot. I need the bike. If I fuck it up I'm theirs. They'll tear me apart and feed me to the giant, who'll grind my bones and make a skin tunic. Or they'll call the police and I'll be returned to my captors and sucked back down the tube. Tiny margins. Watching through hedges as they self-medicate in plain sight. Everything unguarded, including the bike.

I try to disguise my limp, biting down on the pain. I don't look like a thief. Thieves are sinewy and lithe. They have beady dark eyes that flick from left to right. I consider smiling. Asking directions. Ask them if they've seen my dog. Ask them if they know the way to the hospital or the police station. Complete the charade.

...Just take the fucking bike...

The handle bars are angled perfectly, 45-degrees to the wall. The bike is love. It's escape. Another night in paradise. No bike, no Ophelia. He'll drag me out front and beat me around the temples as my blood splatters his yellow flip-flops and he kicks me into the road.

She won't wait for me. She'll move on, just like that. They always do. They're never alone for long. Not the pretty ones. It'll be me that suffers. And then what? Jump into another underpass. Walk into the sea.

Stop threatening things no one cares about. You slept-walked into this moment, you lummox. Like you've done your whole fucking miserable stupid life. So take the bike and ride it to Ray's and be grateful that you still have options because the world owes you fuck all.

They're slow to react. Stoned. Eyes and mouths wide with anger and disbelief. The dog yelps as the mug smashes.

"Oi!"

Hands on, leg over and balance as the chain slips and cheap gears crunch through the rusty derailleur with all my weight. Slow. Too slow. I haven't ridden a bike in years. Just keep going. Everything you have.

I feel a hand tug on the saddle, fingertips at my shoulder. Then he lets go, tumbling to the floor with a hard slap as I pump the unfamiliar pedals. Clicks and squeaks. Down the curb and into the road. The satisfying whirr of rubber tyres on a new surface. Voices behind me and the clap-clap-clomp of flat indecisive feet, as the rushing air cools my skin and dries my brow.

*

Deep in the undergrowth an old man masturbates furiously a few yards away from my face. How long for I don't know. I hid the bike and fell asleep. But regardless when I woke he was there, cock out, humming and muttering breathlessly over the images in his head. The bangles on his wrist jangling like a Christmas sleigh.

Slap, slap, slap. Jangle, jangle, jangle.

He cums and grunts with satisfaction.

“Spying on me were you, you little shit!”, he croaks with a pronounced lisp. “Like watching, do you? Dirty little cunt.”

I try and move. Try and kneel, thinking of escape, but my leg buckles beneath me.

“Don’t go. Just stay a little while. Have a drink with me. Does wonders for the pain.”

There’s a wild look in his eye. A madness. His front teeth are missing and his face is a weathered squash of brown wrinkles, earlobes drooping under the weight of several rusted safety pins. All dressed in mauve. There’s some Indian in him perhaps. He sits down beside me and pulls out a bottle of Amaretto, pouring some into a delicate china teacup.

“Drink it. It’s good. Keeps me warm", he says.

I do as he says before he snatches the sticky cup away from me.

“Not all of it! It’s Doobie’s!”

“Who’s Doobie?”, I ask.

“Me! Stupid! Everyone knows that.”

Grinning. Brown teeth. No teeth. Pierced tongue. Eyebrow. Nose. He reaches into his bag and takes out a pack of well-thumbed playing cards. Photographs from the 70’s. Tanned men. Some naked. Others in fluffy knitwear and polo necks. All athletic with bright white teeth. All Proudly erect. Doobie licks his lips and removes the rubber band.

“Can you play snap?”

He splits the pack and hands me half, laying down his first card with series of grunts, tongue out. He lays down a six. I lay down a two. He lays down an eight. I lay down a three. He lays down a Queen. I lay down a Queen.

"Snap!!! Snap, snap, snap, snap, snap, snap. Clap, clap, clap, clap, clap... I win 'cause I'm the King. Do you want to play again?"

"Okay."

"I don't. I hate snap. Snap's crap!"

He shoves the cards back in his bag and takes another swig from the cup. None for me this time.

"I have to go", I say.

"Where?"

"Home."

"Noooo! Please!", he yells, hands clasped like a beggar.

"Don't leave me here! Not on my own. I can't get home. Take me with you! Please! Back to your house."

"I can't, it's not allowed."

"Says who?"

"Clive."

"Clive's a cunt", he hisses.

"Do you know Clive?"

"I know everything. Ask me a question." But he doesn't let me. Just flushes red. "Mind your own business. It's got nothing to do with you. Weren't hurting nobody."

It's like he's talking to someone else. Someone I can't see or hear. I'm running out of time. I have to go. I need to make Ray's before he closes. Everything hurts. Ankles and knees.

"Don't go! You can't leave me here with them. Chew your face off they will. Eat your dick. Live in the sewer-pipes. Have you seen them?"

"No."

"I 'ave. Sea monsters."

I ask him where.

"In the fucking sea, of course! Gobbles up all the junkies. Loves the taste of Junkie-blood. Bitter like Campari. Eats 'em whole. Crunch! Crunch! Crunch! Crunch! Crunch! Crunch. And the Sea-Apes."

"Sea-Apes?"

"Yeah. Big fucking pink things with huge wanking hands. It's the drink, you see. Raping little bastards. Eating fox meat with their fingers. Everything you don't think's possible, is. This is just the surface, this shit. This ain't it. It's just the skin bit. The good stuff's underneath. The magic and all that. You have to dig for it. Don't dig, don't find."

Doobie looks me up and down, doe-eyed.

"You should see the unicorn. Glows in the dark. Big horn. Right out the centre of its head like a cock. Keep your eyes open, boy. You'll see it if you look hard enough. You see things no one else sees, don't ya boy? It's in your eyes. Must really hurt. Here..."

Doobie hands me the bottle like a tavern drunk, and I drink the spirit like it's water.

"Plenty more where that came from. Drink it all down. Every night I feeds the unicorns. I can show you if you like. Down on the East Beach. After midnight."

"Where's the East Beach?"

"East, you stupid cunt", he says, yawning like a cat.

"I need to go now. Need me sleep. You wanna come? I'll suck you off."

"I've got someone", I say.

"You ain't got no one, boy. Everyone knows that. Love's the great disease. Drives 'em mad, boy. Ain't no one safe."

Knowing eyes, breaking character. Like the universe is talking to me through him. Like they sent him to find me and watched as I crawled into the plants with my stolen pushbike, and sent him in to serve up some home truths with his dick in his hand.

"What are you fucking looking at?", he screams. "Show me your cock or get out of my house!" Then he's gone. The trampled clearing suddenly empty. Maybe he does have the answers. Maybe he's the truth and everything else is just lies.

*

Ray hurries me through the shop to a partially furnished sitting room and kitchenette. There's a black leather sofa piled with junk and a small red portable TV. It stinks of fags. In the corner, across the back door, is a stack of bikes covered over with dust sheets and blankets.

"Did anyone see you?"

“No”, I lie. He takes out his wallet and peels off two ten-pound notes.

"How was that?", he asks.

"Easy."

"Good man."

“Where’s the landfill?", I ask him.

“Out by the barracks. But stick to nicking, son, believe me. It’s dangerous down there. It’ll make you ill.”

“I’m not a thief”, I say.

“We’re all thieves”, he replies. “You’ll realise that soon enough.”

*

A television hums and mumbles from the room off the hotel reception, blue with fag smoke. There’s something scraping in my leg. In my knee joint. Bone or cartilage. I hand Clive the money Ray gave me. He smells it and smiles.

“Same time tomorrow”, he says with a snarl.

He knows my game. Worked me out long ago. The second I walked in through the door probably. I stand there a while too long admiring him. His strong jaw and weathered skin. He’s a man alright. Like men should be. Maybe he knows. Maybe he’s in on it. Why else would he let me stay here? The universe brought me here and Clive let me stay.

“Oi, I’m talking to you!”, he barks.

He could just hand the money back. Put me on the street in the cold. Unable to walk. Never to set foot inside Hotel Ophelia again. He has that power. But he's saving me for later. Perhaps he needs me.

Perhaps I mean something to him. Something I don't know. Shut up. Sit still. Play by the rules and maybe, just maybe, there'll be a room here for you this time tomorrow. Ray was right. We are all thieves. Play the game. Don't rattle the bars. He doesn't need your money.

Love's the ultimate luxury. A luxury I can't afford.

Upstairs Sam's waiting by the door. "You okay?"

"I need to rest", I say weakly, feeding her instinct to mother.

I want to ask her about Clive and the hotel but don't. I can't assume loyalty even if she is washing my clothes and buying me food and tending my wounds like a battlefield medic. She could be one of them.

I lie on the bed and she examines me, her hands cold against my hot swollen knee.

"You should get that looked at."

"I can't."

"Why not?"

"It's not broken."

"You don't know that."

"I walked back."

"I'll get you a bandage."

She reaches for the door handle and pulls away with a yelp. A trickle of blood pools at her knuckle and she stares at the tip of a screw sticking through the doorframe.

“Fuckin’ death-trap”, she says, sucking her finger and shutting the door behind her.

*

Ophelia’s shouting. Angry. Angry with me and angry with them. She hates to see me hurt, but says I brought it on myself. I let her say her piece. Screaming problems without offering solutions. But she’s not the one risking life and limb. She’s not out here in the world. In the cold. In the rain.

My knees buckle and lock. There’s an ache in my guts. She’s the foundation stone. The glue that holds me together. The good bit. She doesn’t need to lift a finger. She could have anyone she wants. I’m a fool. Like before with Clive. If I don’t have her I have nothing. It all dies.

But what if this is what she does? Weary travelers. Haunting their dreams. Waking them up. Hypnotising and enchanting them with her poisonous orange light. Watching as they rise up like entranced cobras and slither across the room. Seduction and deception like a Siren. Maybe the real enemy’s in this room. Deliver me to evil. Perhaps I’ve got this all wrong.

What if there’s nowhere she can’t see me? What if she’s not one room? What if she’s every room or the whole building? Everyone in every room. Fucking everyone. Floating through the hotel unnoticed, room to room to room. Injecting herself into shadows and dust, hanging in the air. A parasite living in light waves and soundwaves. Radio waves. Occupying her own frequency.

Still she shouts. Maligning and belittling. Lucy never treated me like this.

I ask her if she deliberately hurt Sam and she just screams louder. So I leave the hotel and walk.

There's no pain in my leg. My heart has taken it, and I walk through the endless wind, replaying what she said, the cruel echo of her voice. Taunting, doubting, criticizing. Always spying. Not arriving with the night and orange light, just pretending to.

I could drift off without fuss or drama. Walk in a straight line or hug the coast. Only myself to worry about. No responsibility for the others I've always been so keen to embrace. Like men and their children, so beloved yet so bemoaned. Just walk and walk and walk until the weather hits and I rest in a ditch and pull my fleece up over my head and let the elements go to work. Reduce me to nothing. Back to the earth like Lucy, until there's no trace.

I could, but I won't.

*

Moonlight on water. A deep sandy beach surrounded on all sides by the long coarse grass and muddy dunes. In the far distance, firelight. Just a dot of orange in the blue dark at the back of the beach by the clay overhang.

"The handsome ones don't normally come", says a voice in the shadows.

Maybe it's another trap. He holds out a bottle of Amaretto and I drink. Careful not to cut my mouth on the smashed supermarket security cap.

"Thirsty, are you boy? I got plenty", he says tapping his string bag. "Doobie's always got plenty."

We sit in silence on the sand looking out at the rolling waves. It's warm in our little cove away from the wind, as the booze heats my chest and cheeks. She can't follow me here.

"Why did you come, boy?", he asks, rocking backwards and forwards.

"To see the Unicorn."

"You don't believe in Unicorns."

He speaks like we have history. Past lives. A love gone sour. Regret and familiarity.

"Where do you live?", I ask him.

"Got fuck all to do with you."

"You asked me to come home with you."

"Then you would have found out."

"I thought you were joking."

"I'm old. I don't have time for jokes."

Doobie lights another cigarette and swigs on his bottle, thick booze dripping off white whiskers like sap in the firelight

"Where are they?"

"They'll be here."

"When?"

"They'll be here", he says again and I lie back on the smooth cold sand and wait.

*

Dawn light. Doobie's gone and the fire's cold. There's a light rain soaking my clothes, almost to the skin, and the same old pain throbs in my knee and head.

A young chestnut Vizla sniffs at my feet then runs in wide circles, looping back excitedly, looking for a game. Its owner cuts a lonely figure further down the beach, shouting, sensing danger, worried for the animal. Too far away to protect it from whoever or whatever I am and the many possible reasons I'm on the beach.

"Skipper! Skipper! Leave the poor man alone."

Skipper runs on, all legs and fat paws. And as they disappear I see the hoof marks in the sand near the water's edge. Hoof marks and footprints.

My feet are hot in my boots and I can still taste booze as I pull another trolley from a ditch a few hundred yards from a giant Asda.

Maybe Doobie's right. Maybe there is magic in this town. Ghosts and devils. Or maybe he's mad and I'm just lost. I missed my shot at death for another shot at love and I thought I'd won. Hit the jackpot. But I was wrong. So death it is.

I'm not ready to go back. I'm hurt and tired. But I'm not giving up on her. Not yet. I need to hear her side. Plus where would I go?

*

Dusty tippers thunder by as the coast yields to a vast table-top expanse of compacted rubbish crowned by bulldozers and excavators, pushing it around like giant Dung Beetles.

Small individual fires burn in the distance sending up thin spirals of black smoke combining like a great grey halo over the whole expanse.

It's too cold for flies but the birds sense something. Thousands of them. Stabbing supermarket bags and oily foil trays with their dirty yellow beaks. Fighting and striking with huge white wings. Survival of the fittest as they feast on baked beans and plant-based baby shit.

One pads over, stamping its feet nervously. Stabbing at the ground with its bloody beak. It wants to kill me. Kill me and eat me. It would happily sit on my belly and pull my guts out through a small incision if it could. Feasting on my organs and drinking my blood. But I'm alive and have hands and it doesn't, so it can't. Instead it sits in wait, hate in its eyes. The evolutionary frustration. Brains beyond its means.

Give it another ten million years. Grow some hands, then we'll see what you're capable of. Because if seagulls had hands we'd be fucked. A savage society of science and violence run by seagulls. Throwback dinosaurs finally taking over despite the meteor. All hail the opposable thumb.

If seagulls had hands we'd all be living on landfills or slums and shanties, queuing for scraps and leftovers, as they gorge on raw salmon in posh restaurants and send probes into space searching for mineral deposits.

If seagulls had hands they'd systematically destroy everything in their path. Rape your wives, eat your kids, burn your churches.

If seagulls had hands we'd all be underground. Digging tunnels deeper and deeper into the earth. Desperate to escape.

Searching for sanctuary. Places they can't follow. As we regroup in secret while they execute their landgrab, overthrowing governments and the military, and destabilising the global economy.

Seagulls with hands in little suits on talk shows interviewing other seagulls with hands about movies and politics. Seagulls with hands with guns patrolling the empty streets as humans cower in basements praying not to be found. Firing missiles at our decaying tower blocks as bodies pile up in the streets, feeding an already dominant army as it grows and grows, big and strong. Slitting throats.

Seagulls with hands feasting on our dead human flesh. Stripping it off our bones. Feasting on our surplus protein. Cooking it over burning oil drums in the smoking debris-filled post-apocalyptic towns and streets.

Giant seagulls, six feet tall, smoking cigarettes and watching German porn on smart phones as great snaking lines of starving human refugees line the outer highways heading north while seagulls with hands holding AK47's pick them off one by one.

Seagull money. Seagull tech. Seagull media. Seagull Gods. Seagull brands. Seagull drugs. Any trace of humanity scrubbed from the history books. But they don't have hands. Not yet. And I do, so I start to dig, one eye on the sky. Looking for signs.

If seagulls had hands...
If seagulls had hands...
If seagulls had hands...
If seagulls had hands...
If seagulls had hands...

It's back-breaking work. Like the strawberry fields in summer. Over-extending. All my weight through my back and knees. Plastic bottles dancing and spinning, toppling over the edges of the hard-packed banks until still, collecting in holes and hollows.

But the worse things get, the easier it is to battle on. Locking the pain away in places I can't see or feel, feeding on it. Turning adversity and struggle into fuel.

In the distance the machines kill and claw and roar in clouds of dust as the birds attack the freshly ploughed surface for carrion and scraps. A brigade of bulldozers and excavators and bailers, wheels the size or cars, belching acrid diesel smoke. Natives of a distant planet, softened by mist, performing the tasks of their overlords.

My fingers bleed from nicks and scratches. Rusty sharps, blades and burnt needles. Broken glass and china. Metal lids. lethal in the wrong hands. Memories of my grandmother keeping half-eaten cans of cheap dogfood in her shopping bag until her Giant Poodle, Rag, sliced its tongue off on a tin of Pal. Told me to hit it with a brick and bury him away from the house. Said she couldn't bear to say goodbye. Said he'd starve to death without a tongue.

The rubbish must be ten metres deep where I'm standing. The secrets it must keep. Just like the sea. Evidence and weapons and fingers and thumbs, gnawed at by bloodthirsty rats desperate for a meal. Like the gulls, but more accustomed. This is what they were born to do. Adapted perfectly to any situation or terrain, from the shit-caked sewers of London to the fresh air of the Essex coast. These little fuckers can deal with it. They'll chew their own legs off to escape, no questions asked. If only it was that easy.

Heat floats off the surface in a fine mist. A bacterial warmth which comforts me. Decomposition and reduction creating and supporting life. If I tunnelled down and set up camp I'd have all I need. Live like a rat. Become one. Become rat. Never see a soul. Just me and the birds fighting it out for the best bits.

Maybe I'll build a scarecrow and wire it with speakers and flashing lights, primed with catapults to keep them away. Establish civilisation on the rich stinking loam of the landfill and live for a thousand years surrounded by my children and grandchildren. Build schools and factories and churches underground as the rubbish piles up on top of us. Ton after ton after stinking ton. Me and the Omega People. All of us.

The machines and their overlords would never find us down there. Too big and cumbersome. Their buckets and caterpillar tracks useless against our ingenuity and desperation to survive and multiply and evolve. Big staring eyes for seeing in tunnels. Huge hands for shoveling earth and rubbish. Thick coarse hair to trap warmth and protect our skin.

I find a small silver crucifix on a grey chain and pick it up to inspect its Latin inscription. Could be worth something. A working medium-wave transistor. Some picture frames. A bloodied five-pound note.

I make six large piles of cans in a square about a hundred yards long, bagged up and tied with string and twine. Piling them high in the trolley and pulling them back to the dirt road. Back and forth, back and forth, back and forth.

In the portacabin an old man sits behind a clean counter reading a paperback, bright new hi-vis at odds with his weather-beaten face and gnarled knuckles.

"Just put them in there, mate", he says pointing at a large basket on top of some digital scales.

I tip the cans into the basket as high as they will go and he presses a button on the front of the scales.

"three-point-six-seven", he says. "That's about four quid. Do you want to fetch the rest?"

That plus a bloodied fiver I found in a bin bag. I do two more trips, my pockets full of trinkets for Ray. Gifts for Ophelia. I'm ready to go back to her. Work it out. My anger's gone and I've stopped hearing her voice in the whistling wind.

*

Ophelia asks me where I've been. No orange light Just daylight. She asks me if I'm okay. Says she's sorry. Says she wasn't spying and didn't hurt Sam, but I don't believe her. I need her more than anything and I don't care that she lied, as long as she's on my side. By my side. I don't care that she's jealous. I don't care about the little girl next door and the constant stream of men Clive escorts to her room, or the immigrant workers waiting for the van.

Clive. Perky. The violence. The suffering.

I don't care about any of it. My life is in this room. The rest is superfluity. I need to focus and harden. I can't save their lives, but I can save mine. They won't thank me. They don't know I'm here. I'm invisible. They need to take responsibility, not me. They came here looking for opportunity and sanctuary. I could have saved them the trip. All they had to do was ask.

"I brought you something", I say emptying my pockets. "God to watch over us. To say I'm sorry. To stop us falling apart. I'm sorry for the things I said."

You don't believe in God, she says.

"I do now", I say as I hang the crucifix from a picture hook above the bed. And seeing it there makes me believe again. Like when I was a boy. She's sorry too. Ashamed of the things she said to me. Called me. The cruel things.

The transistor hisses, like air being released as sounds and structures emerge. A rhythm, sharpening to something robust and up-tempo like Samba.

"I'm sorry for doubting you."

I strip and we start to move. Swaying and arching our backs. Robots. Clowns. Sweating. Bouncing around the room, laughing like children, falling naked into each other's arms. Reconciled. Forgiven. Hot. Sweaty. Horny. Fucking hard against the wall, against the floor, to the radio as it spits out tune after tune after tune.

Our courtship is over. No more meeting up shyly in the dark, hiding in the orange glow, flattering my body and face with shadow. We're together in the light. Nowhere to hide. Naked and exposed. Everything was rushed. We moved too fast.

Declaring love, our hearts breaking when we were apart. Living for when we were together. It burns out. The arguments. Pressure. I see that now. We needed time apart. Which is why I stayed out on the beach with the unicorns and came back bearing gifts. So now we must seamlessly transition. No glow. No best version of ourselves. Just us. The two of us. As we are.

She kisses me, wraps herself around me and leads me to the bed. This is what it was all for. The hard work and the early starts. The wet and the cold. Pain and fatigue. Wounds and infection and illness. Not knowing if it's the last day or the first of many more. Rolling the dice. This is what it's all been for. For this. However brief.

VII.

Janet sits at one end of a large oval table in a stuffy beige meeting room, Mary Parsons facing her.

Mike was in New York. The house was hers. No dreading him coming home. No difficult dinner requests. Things that take a whole afternoon to prepare, for him to just get in late half-drunk having already eaten somewhere nice. No kiss, no thanks, no nothing.

She always wanted to be married. Mike didn't. Said it didn't mean anything to him but she was adamant. Any children would be born in wedlock with Mike or without. So she gave him an ultimatum and he gave in. Probably the last time he did. Maybe he resented her for it. There were arguments. She remembers those, but then the children came along and it was like that old life belonged to someone else.

She remembers watching him on their wedding day. It was just a piss-up to him. Turned up stinking of gin. Him and his water-skiing friends. Going through the motions. The vows. All the right things in all the right places but his heart wasn't in it. She knew that but didn't blame him. If it wasn't what he wanted he was making a huge sacrifice for her. Which was out of character. So it must have meant something, but exactly what she never found out.

She cried that night as he passed out beside her and wet the bed in his wedding suit, something they never mentioned again. The reasons behind it.

Anxiety maybe. Fear. Secrets. More things never to discuss. Just add it to the list. Left to raise her kids in a comfortable emotional vacuum.

Of course, he was screwing everything that moved. She knew that. She had eyes and ears and a sense of smell. She found things. The clichés. Receipts. Numbers scribbled on matchbooks. Business cards. Later, text messages and stray emails. He'd have late nights in London and say he was staying in a hotel. Always nicer to her when he got home. Not much, but enough to notice.

Golfing weekends with clients or city friends she'd never heard of. To Spain and Portugal. He had three phones. But she had the boys and that was enough and when they grew up she had the people who needed her help. People like Sam.

"We're running a bit behind so we need to keep this relatively brief", is the first thing that comes out of Mary's pinched little mouth. "I've read your report, but I see no obvious reason to change things. She's doing well. The child is settled with her foster carers. But I need to see more evidence Samantha's ready to look after Jody independently again."

"She's been there for six months. She needs a place of her own", says Janet.

Mary frowns at the interruption. "But you said yourself she's not ready to look after the child. Has she been applying for jobs? You mentioned college last time. Has there been any progress there?"

"Not as far as I know", Janet says, conceding the point.

"Have you asked her? That is your job, Janet."

"I know what my job is, Mary. She hasn't applied yet, no."

"Well maybe she should."

"We've discussed it and she wants to concentrate on Jody and her sobriety while she's in temporary accommodation. She feels she wouldn't be able to commit to a vocational course in her current circumstances. But, in my opinion, she is more than ready to start leading an independent life."

"The onus is on her to make the necessary steps. We can't rebuild her life for her."

"Those places are zoos."

"Those *zoos* provide very a necessary overspill. We have an acute housing shortage."

"Because too many low-priority cases are treated as high priority cases."

"We can't separate children and parents without good cause."

"But you're keeping Sam and Jody apart?"

"Because she has a history of substance abuse and neglect. Not because we're prioritising other cases."

Janet reddens.

"And do you think that place is helping her mental state? I've got to sit down with her now and explain that absolutely nothing's going to change. That her daughter stays with the family and she remains stuck in an overcrowded B&B with a growing reputation for poor standards, which we all seem happy to turn a blind eye to because - let's face it - there's nowhere else for her to go. And there's no more money in the housing budget because the council wants to clean up a beach that no one ever goes on, in a town that no one ever comes to because it's full of undesirables we can't house."

"Have you finished?", asks Mary.

Janet sits back in her seat arms folded, regretting the suit and the outburst. This is government. There's no place for emotion or a personal sense of injustice. She knew better than to let her temperature rise in these cold still rooms.

"So what happens now?", asks Janet, calming herself down.

"We'll review her case in six months."

"Six months?"

"Now can we move on?"

"It's like you want her to fail."

Mary puts her hands together as her chest flushes pink below a silver teardrop necklace.

"The decision has been made. So let me offer you a word of advice. Don't get emotionally involved with your clients. It really doesn't suit you."

She makes a note in her notepad and one in the case notes leaving Janet nowhere to go but out.

*

Alma smells blood in the water a couple of miles away. Salty and ferric. Just enough to shake her from sleep, half-buried in silt. It means there's a package. Sailed in from Holland and switched to one of the cockle boats in the North Sea, as the fleet returned with its quota.

The Dutch boat returning clean as the skipper of the Anne Marie hooks the bag to a buoy a couple of miles from shore. Even if they search it they'll find nothing. They're too clever for that. The technology's too advanced. Cleverer than the dogs. Dogs aren't clever. Just grinning idiots with keen noses.

Each batch is a 5kg freeze-dried slab of refined cocaine. Vacuum packed and double bagged in heat-sealed industrial-strength plastic wallets, with just enough buoyancy to float six inches below the surface unnoticed. Ready to be unshackled and dragged to shore on her belly. Any heavier and it would slow her down. She was weak. All junkies are weak.

Each slab chipped by the gang to monitor its progress from the boat. If she moves in the wrong direction they'll come back and kill her, assume she's working for someone else. If she loses it she'll be punished. But it's a low-risk strategy. The only real threat coming from rogue mermaids working for rival gangs, but in all her time working for Clive there'd never been a problem.

If she died mid-job they'd dredge the bottom for the package and her body to avoid suspicion from government agents combing the beaches disguised as dog-walkers and metal detectorists. They didn't want her dead, but neither did they want a global furore.

This was her river. Her sea. Why would anyone come looking for mermaids in the Thames Estuary?

She drives up through the water at incredible speed, registering temperature and light changes, her head its usual fog of withdrawal. She loves him with an intensity she can't explain, maintaining her half-life in the deep polluted waters waiting for the call. Either from the drug boats, or if business is slow and the heat was on, Coco herself.

If only she could walk out of here, but she can't. If only she could lie in Coco's bed. But it was hopeless. Another impossible lopsided fucked-up love. But love was love. And love is what every girl wants.

She unties the parcel and pulls it a few feet under the water out of sight of the cockle boats chugging off into the mist, then swims it quickly and silently towards the pontoon where she waits for the put-put-put of the tiny outboard engine.

*

Beauty wasn't something Janet ever had to worry about. She certainly never needed to downplay it. Mike was really the first person to notice her. Maybe there'd been others, but boys and girls don't talk do they. They just sit alone fantasising about what candour and honesty might feel like.

She smiles at the thought as Sam skips down the hotel steps. She's a girl. Moves like a girl. The coat she hides in. Her greasy scraped-back hair. No make-up. Beauty's a burden in places like these.

Now Janet has to break her heart again. It's already there in her body language. If it was good news she'd be out of the car already, all smiles. But it's not good news.

Sam gets in with the familiar rustle and fresh fag stink as Janet shuts her eyes and takes a breath.

"Look, I'm not going to beat around the bush. It's bad news I'm afraid." Sam stares ahead with wet eyes. "They rejected your application."

"Are you taking the fucking piss?!"

Her head drops and her fingers claw and clench. Tears.

"They think you need more time."

"More time? More time for what?"

"There'll be other reviews. You'll get it at the next one I promise. I'll make sure of it."

"When?"

"Six months."

"Are you joking? I can't. I've had enough."

She grabs angrily at the door handle and walks, shoulders hunched, up the road. Janet jumps out and calls after her.

"Sam!"

"Leave me alone!!"

Screaming, running, sobbing up the street.

Janet resists the urge to follow. It's not her job. She's not her mother. So she just watches her go, knowing full well what's about to happen.

*

The tiny Indian woman takes Sam's money and hands her the bottle. They'd grown close without really speaking. Her and the girl in the big black puffy coat. Just polite hellos and thankyous and goodbyes as she bought rolling tobacco and papers. But she'd never seen her cry and she'd never seen her drink. It was none of her business.

She wasn't here to tell people how to live. They'd be out of business. The mark-up on addiction was huge.

Sam takes her change, looking up to the CCTV and the convex anti-theft mirror at the far end of the tightly packed shop, next to the bread and cereal. Then out to the piss-stinking alley behind two wheelie bins and a waterlogged sofa. The vodka's hot on her breath. Like the past six months never happened.

She feels warm and slow, stood on the damp uneven ground behind the shops and bins. She can smell the sea and the fags on her fingers. Fried onions and bacon. She can hear the rush of daytime traffic. Off and running. Back for another.

Don't fuckin' judge me bitch. Just take my fucking money.

Not drunk, just taking it all in. Fresh eyes. Old friend. Where she left off. She wants to chain smoke cigarettes. Gorge and binge. Run and run. She wants night to come and swallow her whole. Sat on a barstool flirting with old boys in the old town and wide boys in the snooker hall.

You don't need the coat no more. Stop covering up. Relax. Have some fun. You're young, for fuck's sake. You're beautiful for fuck's sake. Put some lippy on. Undo a button. Have a fucking day off. You can't spend your life pretending, ploughing some bullshit virtuous furrow. You're a drunk, girl. Pure and fucking simple. Ain't nothing you can do about it. Sitting around in them groups chatting shit. Patting yourself on the back. Listening to their miserable little sob stories. Sober drunks at a party with no booze, that's all that is. The worst fucking party in the world. And it counts for shit 'cause no one cares, mate. No one gives a fuck. Just you lot. Huddled together, terrified of yourselves. You're young, so just be what you are. You've got time.

"Double vodka and Diet Coke", she says to the girl behind the bar. It feels good. She feels free. Free to choose. Free to just walk into a bar and order a drink. Like the old days. Before Jody. Before everything collapsed.

"'Three-eighty please", says the barmaid placing the glass on the rubber drip-mat.

Sam tops it up with the vodka from her pocket. The world wide open, not closed. She's in a game, jumping from level to level, world to world. Capable of anything. She knows where it ends. But while there's daylight and a way back she'll take it hour by hour.

The upstairs bar is empty apart from a couple of old pissheads with blue tattoos. Double doors lead off to a pool room with four tables, strip-lit by black plastic canopies hanging from the ceiling.

She drapes her coat over a stool. Her phone keeps ringing. It's Janet. But she's not interested. Janet can fuck off. This is all her fault. She's just trying to make herself feel better. Ease the guilt. Interfering bitch with her comfortable little bullshit life. On some sanctimonious mission to save the poor from themselves.

She promised. They did it all her way. And look how it ended up. Back to the fucking start. She can't do it no more. Not there. Another six months hiding herself away while the evil theatre plays out below. She hasn't the energy. It's all gone. She needs this. Maybe tomorrow we go again but give me today. She hears her name, sees a familiar face.

"Sam. What you doing here?" She's pleased to see him. To see anyone. "I thought you were behavin' yourself."

"What's that mean?", she says smiling, tongue between her teeth.

He laughs and looks at his feet. Paul was a friend of Craig's. One of the lads. He used to come round and play computer games and smoke weed. A couple of years older, maybe less. He worshipped Craig. They all did. Dressed like him. Talked like him. Wanted to be him. And she loved being around all of them. Craig's kid sister. Fit as fuck. She had that thing they all wanted, teasing them in her little pink shorts. Flirting with them in front of Craig down the football club. Look but don't touch.

Paul was quieter than the others. He was the butt of a lot of jokes. Tall and skinny with a big nose. Just happy to be there. Then at the funeral they sat around trestle tables drinking flat pints and watched it all die.

"Good to see you, Paul."

She shuffles slightly in her seat, backing into him, letting him smell her.

"You want another drink?", he asks.

"Yeah, go on then. But I can't afford to get you one back."

"It's fine. I'm back working. Security guard up London now", he says rocking on his heels. Swag.

"Drinks are on you then", she giggles, hanging her arm off his hip, brushing his flank gently with her fingertips. He leans into her and whispers, glancing at the door.

"I've got a bit of gear on me if you fancy a line. Might make a day of it." Anything to make her stay. He presses a bag into her palm and she closes her fingers tight.

"Have you got a note?", she says and he hands her a tenner, looking around to see who's watching.

It's a full gram. A bit rocky.

She bangs two line off the top of the toilet roll dispenser, rubbing the leftovers on her gums. Another line – *bang*. Smaller. Greedy. Suddenly aware of the music from the bar as the chemicals hit her blood and brain. That sour taste and a numbness on the roof of her mouth. Bleach and detergent.

It'll all have to be paid for. But being without seems scarier. If she went home now she'd be up for hours, just herself for company, chain smoking rollies. She needs to keep climbing. She'll walk back out there and drink her drink and dangle Paul for as long as it takes.

Back in the bar she presses the wrap into his palm. Gives him that look. The drug look. Complicity. There's a sudden sourness on his breath. Fags and lager.

"Thanks mate", she says. She could have called him *babe* or *hun* but she called him *mate*. Kicked the door shut. The more you spend the more you get.

She'd be putting out in a few hours, he knew that as much as anyone. And he wasn't in any rush. He'd just come off twenty nights straight, up and down to Moorgate. He'd hardly seen daylight. It was his first day out in weeks.

Rent paid, two grand in the bank, cash in his pocket. She had fuck all, he knew that. He knew all about the kid and the authorities.

Okay, she wasn't seventeen anymore but things were different now. Buyer's market. She needed him. Why else was she here, sitting on a bar stool on her own in the middle of the day? If this was the end of the longest long game in history, he'd played a blinder. Wasn't even worried about money. This was the best day of his life so far. Craig was a bully anyway.

They sit thinking about the accident, sipping their drinks in silence.

"Do you ever see the others?", she asks.

"Not really. Dickson got married, didn't he. Glenn met some bird in Australia. I don't know what Justin's doing. Went up London. Finsbury Park way, I 'fink."

He pauses. "You look good, Sam."

"Thanks", she says and looks away. "So do you."

He smiles bashfully.

"Do you see your mum much?"

"No."

"You had a kid didn't ya?"

"Yeah."

"You not with the dad then?"

“He fucked off”, she says turning back to face him. "Turned out to be a cunt."

*

Slow motion now. Pumping pounds into the juke box. Pumping sounds. Old school anthems. Bitter sweet symphonies. Memories of youth and freedom. Sunny days and Strongbow. Blow jobs and love. Crumbling solid and smoking weed.

The bar’s filling up. Night falling. Daytime drinkers getting swallowed by a new crowd. Workers with black calloused hands and ripped jackets with polyester wadding and tartan linings. Paint-splattered and scuffed. Dark faces misshapen by graft and poor diet and fags and booze. Pain and trauma.

Cheap consolatory pints, while Sam and Paul disappear further down their tunnel.

Her phone battery’s dead. All she has is Paul. The two of them, conspicuous in the corner. Clumsy movements. Spilt drinks. Eyes spinning as they kiss and fondle. Attracting attention. Smirks and nods.

He’s got his hands between her legs. He’s licking her neck and ear. His stinking breath right in her face. The room’s hot and noisy and small. Condensation on the glass. Great roars of laughter. Talk of sex and football and Brexit. Protect our borders. Keep the immigrants out. Harry Kane. He’s one of our own.

She needs to leave. Get out. Where did she put her coat? But she can’t go home. She’s fucked. He’s shouting. Gurning. Face twisting and turning. In and out of focus. He don’t care about Craig now. Looking and fucking touching. Horny little bastard. Big time security guard, now. A boner for graft. A boner for her. She can see it. Feel it through his jeans. Who is she? Where is she?

"We all fucking fancied you", he screams in her ear. There, he finally said it, after all those years. Thinks he can. Thinks he's in. It's him. She recognises him. He was mates with her brother. Where's her brother? Is he here?

"I was just a kid."

"So?"

"I used to fancy all of yous", she lies.

"You should have said something."

"Yeah. But, you know."

She doesn't want to think about Craig or how things were. That's not what today's about. Her day off too, from 'what ifs' and self-blame. Not a day goes by. She's about to cry. He's taken her there. Him and the booze. Fucked it without knowing. Fucked everything. He was so close.

"'I've got a bottle of vodka at home if you wanna go back."

"You got any more gear?"

"Loads. And I can get more."

She'll do the coke, fuck him and go. But she's not going home. She needs the night to last forever. She needs to go places. See people. Fuck more people if need be. This can't end.

They stagger down the sticky rubber-topped stairs and out into the sudden night air. His hands are all over her. On her arse and tits. She's super alert now. Like her ears and eyes are the same thing. He kisses her properly, jabbing his hard-on into her stomach as they lean against a wall to stay upright.

"Let's get a cab", she says, pulling him over to the rank.

It's 9 o'clock. Feels like midnight. The night is young. Too young. They climb into the back of a Silver Citroen and kiss as she swigs from the forgotten bottle of Chekhov. 9pm. She has all night and all morning and she knows all the places to go.

*

Dusty laminate flooring. A flat-screen television and a PS4 wrapped in its own cables. An ironing board in the lounge. The faintest smell of stale bed linen and sweat. She can hear the scrape of the drawers and the crunch of ice as he pours drinks and knocks things over.

"You got any wine?", she shouts through to the back. She wants to taste something. Something other than vodka. Wine will tip her over as it settles in her empty guts. She knows that much.

She needs a shit.

He appears with the drinks, banging them down on the pine-topped coffee-table, covered in burns and stains. He pours a tumbler of wine and she drinks half of it down as he tosses the rest of the coke on the table and disappears into his bedroom. Returning with another baggie and some pills. Big-time security guard. Big-time Charlie. Multiple tunnels to fall down. She's felt so little for so long, for fear of feeling anything

Fuck Jody. She wants more drugs. Maybe tonight, or at dawn as the workers crawl from their warm clean burrows. She doesn't know where she'll be by then. She could be in the back of a strange car, or in a dark flat surrounded by strange faces speaking in tongues. In a back bedroom. Whatever.

Paul thumbs a pill between her lips, onto her tongue. He takes his with neat vodka from the freezer, thick and syrupy.

"These things don't hang about", he says. His voice is deep and far away. Her neck weak, head heavy. She just wants to sit for a while, the comforting softness of corduroy at her fingertips.

He leans over and kisses her. She kisses him back with a flick of the hard tip of her tongue.

"You got any fags?", she asks.

"Have a line first."

He hands her a fiver. The plastic note scratches the inside of her nose. He does the same and takes a pill she doesn't know about. She can taste blood.

"I really like you", he says, taking her glass out of her hand.

"Can you put some music on?"

"Stop changing the subject!"

"I'm not."

"Come on. We know why we're here."

She feels sick. Acid sick, like something's burning inside her.

"What do you want?", he says flipping through some CD's.

"Anything."

The word lasts forever, bouncing off the thin walls and back to her. There's that sickness. A compulsion to run. For it all to be alright again. To undo what's done.

Everything's dark and getting darker. Just the light from a fish-tank she hadn't noticed. He's on her now, sick of waiting, clumsily pawing at her jeans, turning them inside out over her shoes. Yanking at her knickers which coil into a tight ball under the sofa.

He picks her up, cupping her buttocks, pulling them apart, and slams her against the wall, banging the back of her head. There's pleasure. She's feeling pleasure. Something familiar. The heat of his body, sweat at his neck. His *Oh, yeah*-ing, over and over.

Oh, yeah, oh, yeah, oh, yeah, like he heard it on the hub and liked it. Thinks she'll like it too. Thinks it's how it's done.

He's trying to concentrate. Trying to get hard, stay hard. Looking at her without resorting to the usual fantasy carousel of women he uses to get things moving. Going deep into his feelings but feeling very little. She's still on that list, but she's not a fantasy anymore so he thinks of someone else. Lauren Goodger or Montana off Love Island.

Nothing's happening. Cocaine and Viagra. It may as well be someone else's dick. He has cramp in his left leg. She's starting to feel heavy. Then he feels her convulse and as he opens his eyes she pukes in his mouth and over his face. Cheap red wine and stinging bile. She falls to the floor, lifeless, foaming. Eyes wide and unblinking as he wretches and curses and thinks about the deposit and whether he'll lose his job.

*

Lights above her. Glowing green and strobing. Distant sirens. The stink of puke. Shouting and beeping. Then the rush of cold air. She thinks she's at an airport, going on holiday. Being taken off the aeroplane.

What did she do? Can she still go? Is she in trouble? Will the plane wait? Where's Jody? Is Jody on the aeroplane? Who's looking after Jody?

Bright white strip-lights. The squeak of feet. A man's face straight above her. Ignoring her. Green Jacket. A radio pinned to his shirt. She can see up his nose. Massive nostrils. Nose hair. Who are you? Why are we here? Where's Craig? Is Craig alive? *Thud*, through the bendy rubber doors. Warmer and warmer. Sinking into the blankets. Where's her coat? Her trousers? Her pants. She's virtually naked. She needs her coat. It's got the vodka in it.

Thud, through another set of rubber doors.

Thud, another.

What happened to the wine? Where's Paul? Can she have a cigarette? You don't understand, I need a cigarette. I need to call my dealer. I can't just stop. It doesn't work like that. It can't wear off. I can't go back. Not now. I had bad news. It's not my fault. Please don't tell anyone. Don't tell Clive. Don't tell Janet. Don't tell the council or those people, whatever their names are, John and thingy. What happened to the music and the bloke?

Thud.

They start working on her. Things in her mouth and ears. Clamping things to her finger, pads on her chest. Shining lights in her eyes. Rolls of blue paper rag. Piss and puke everywhere.

They keep asking her name. *What's your name love? Can you tell us what your name is? Who were you with, love? Have you taken anything? How much have you had to drink? Where do you live, love? Is there anyone we should tell?*

The air's thin and cold. Exhaust fumes. Her ears are blocked, only picking up certain sounds. She's sick in a cardboard bowl, saliva and snot hanging off her chin and nose. And she can taste cocaine and blood as they jam a plastic pipe down her neck and into her guts.

*

Two miles away the police are asking Paul questions. Writing things in their notebooks. Staring at him as he comes up on the second pill. The secret one. Dirty little bastard. They know what's happened. It happens every day. Cheap thrills. Cheap drugs. House doubles. *Kiss me quick, fuck me slow.*

It wasn't supposed to be like this. Why does everything end badly? Confidence maybe. A lack of. He loved Sam when they were kids. Like, really loved her. Silently, secretly. Sat in his room, gripping his pillow. It was never about sex, it was love. She was a goddess. And Craig kept it that way. Kept her away. Untouchable. Beyond reach.

Now he can taste her stomach acid in the back of his throat.

'Tell us what happened", says the policeman.

He can feel it, rising from his chest into his head. Weightless. Everything green and slow.

"Did she take anything?"

"I dunno."

"That's not what you told the paramedics..."

Their voices sound distant.

"...I told them what I thought she'd taken." He's flying. Trying hard to focus. He feels sick. "We were just in the pub. When I said I didn't know her, I know her a bit from ages ago."

"Why did you lie?"

"I dunno."

"What's her name?"

"Sam."

“Sam what?”

“Clarke.”

“So what happened?”

“I’m not feeling good.”

“Tell me exactly what happened, Paul. It’s important.”

“She was having some kind of fit so I called 999. Is she going to be okay? I’ve just started a new job. Will I lose my job?”

“Did you have sex with her?”

“No. Yeah. Sort of.”

"Did you or not?"

"I couldn’t, okay. I swear to fucking God!"

He starts to cry like a boy.

“But you didn’t give her anything? Put anything in her drink or anything like that?”

“No!”

“Was she awake when you had sex with her?”

“Course she fucking was!”, he says then vomits on the pavement as the police woman steps back from the deep red splatter.

VIII.

Janet strokes the thin soft skin on the top of Sam's hand as she sleeps. Just a child. Look at her.

She can hear snatches of chatter from around the other beds, above the hum. *'The dogs miss you' and 'when we get you home'*. She doesn't know who these people are or what they look like, but she paints pictures. If they've been through anything similar they'll be desperate, hoping for miracles and new beginnings.

Talking too loudly, like they don't know how to talk or what to say. Family secrets and problem daughters. Self-harm and depression. Gutted fathers unable to cope but having to. Not sure how to be. Remembering when she was born. So small and innocent. Daddy's little girl. If only he'd been there more. Left less of it to her mum. Less time boozing and chasing other women. Younger and fitter.

Burying themselves in football and newspapers and beer. Because their duty stops with the money. Put the food on the table and you can do what you want. That's how it works, right? Right?

There are screens and wooden laminate everywhere. Everything's light and bright. Rubberised and round-edged. On wheels. Hi-tech apparatus with wires and cables coiled up in custom wire baskets. She brought flowers and had the nurse put them in a plastic vase. Clothes and some other bits and bobs she thought she'd need. Toiletries and a floral robe from a hotel in Hong Kong.

Sam opens her eyes and focuses on Janet sitting watching her without reaction, as if she knew she was there.

"Hello, sleepy head", Janet says softly, intimately.

"What are you doing here?", Sam croaks, clearing her throat.

"Just making sure you're okay. How are you feeling?"

Sam smiles, her hair tumbling across the white pillow. She looks perfect and serene. Like a body lying in state. "Terrible."

"You really went for it."

"Yeah."

"Do you want some water?"

"Please."

Sam pulls herself up the pillows and Janet holds a plastic beaker to her lips with a paper straw.

"My breath must stink."

Janet smiles and gestures to an overnight bag. "There's toothpaste and a toothbrush in there."

Sam squeezes Janet's hand and breathes deeply, a wet crackle in her chest.

"Go on then. Get it over and done with."

"What?"

"The bollocking."

"There's no *bollocking*."

Tears well in Sam's tired eyes. She'd never heard Janet swear before. It felt funny and wrong. Janet was the only person who'd ever made her feel safe and loved. Really loved. She didn't need to swear. She had it all. There was no weakness on show or tell. She fought for what's right without expression. She was a constant, made of metal.

Sam took advantage of her sometimes, sure. She'd become a safety net. Sam knew she'd be there. Was it manipulation? Surely just instinct. Nothing evil of cynical.

She'd been doing it all her life. You do down here, to survive. Boys and men. The dole. Clive. Dangling them on bits of string. Making them believe. She worked it out early and never looked back. Until Jody was born and everything changed.

Janet was more like a mum though. The mum she wished she'd had maybe.

"I can't do it anymore", says Sam, her hands around her raised knees. Janet takes a deep breath, the room suddenly very quiet. Just the sound of people listening, shifting uncomfortably in creaking chairs and voices further down the corridor. The constant thud of plastic doors and the ping of the lift.

"I want you to come and live with us", says Janet, gripping Sam's wet hand.

Sam shakes her head from side to side. "I can't."

"Just until you're strong enough. You won't get better there. It's impossible."

"It's not your problem."

"What did they think was always going to happen?" Janet lowers her voice to a whisper.

"They should be ashamed themselves."

"You'll lose your job."

"I don't need the job. You can't stay where you are."

"And I can't live in some mansion either."

"It's not a mansion."

"You know what I mean. Everyone waiting for me to fuck up."

"It wouldn't be like that. You could have died. I'm not sitting back and watching that happen."

Sam starts to sob, no attempt to hide or wipe away her tears. She's past that. Janet slips onto the bed next to her, cradling her in her arms. It feels so good. Her heat. Her hair. Her skinny shoulders. Like a daughter.

"Look, Jody can come too when you get her back. We could go right now. There's nothing stopping you. Get out of here. Start again. Go to college. We'd support you until you're back on your feet."

"No."

"I'll lend you the money for a flat. Let me do it."

"Why?"

"Please."

Sam rests her head on Janet's shoulder. The desperation of everything and the offer she'll have to turn down. Fairyland. Nothing more. People like her didn't live with people like them. Like some strange second childhood in someone else's house. Someone else's world. Then what?

“They’re letting me out tomorrow they said”, says Sam.

Janet strokes her hair. “Have a think and we can go over it tomorrow. We have the room. It’s there whenever you want it.”

*

A rock glances the back of my head and I fall to my knees, blood running into my eyes and dripping off my chin. Flecks and splatter then a stinging heat. Another rock lands nearby, rattling a can. Then another and another. I want to sleep but I'm under attack. Right here in my trench.

In the distance a being or beast, like a minotaur in silhouette, wearing a black crash helmet, clad in layer upon layer of old clothing and rags, stands tall and resolute. Covered in paint. A battle cry of silence chilling me to the bone. I’m in shock. This creature, emerging from the rubble and refuse bound in tape and covered in paint. Whatever it is, it wants me dead.

Hot fresh blood on my hand and between my fingers. I can smell it and taste it. This is a battle to the death. Last man standing. If I leave I die. If I stay I have a chance. But I need to arm up.

Strategise. Mobilise. Retreat.

Still the rocks rain down as I abandon my position and crawl to the less fertile edge of the landfill, and the patches I’ve already worked. Let it have its victory. Let it celebrate in drink. I’ll be back when you least expect it Paintman.

Then we'll fight to the death.

*

I make back to the hotel, dizzy, dirty and bloodied.

Ophelia's waiting in the shadows like a giant scorpion, gathered in, crouched and camouflaged. Full of scorn. I can hear her breathing as her many eyes study my every move, from all angles.

I witch on the transistor radio and start to move in time, swaying as I undress. I feel sexy. Gathering pace. Out of time. New moves. Old moves. Stripping to get her in the mood. But she ignores me.

"Would you like to dance with me? Please dance with me. Why won't you dance with me?"

She doesn't move, just glares with all her eyes, blinking independently.

"FUCKING DANCE WITH ME!"

She tells me to *fuck off*. Not interested. Thinks it's funny. Sits there laughing. Goading. *You look ridiculous. Fat and stupid. You stink. You disgust me.* Then goes back to whatever she was doing. Fingering herself, thinking about Clive. Imagining him fucking her. Stiff as a stick. Hung like a hippo. A giant hippo. A hippo fucking a scorpion. So big she can barely hold it together. Intense pleasure and intense pain as he nudges her guts with it, bruising her kidneys.

Looking down I see Lucy's ashes scattered across the carpet.

She said she didn't mind. We had an agreement. No secrets. She said she understood.

"You said you understood. You knew what she meant to me. She's the reason I'm here. The reason we're together. I watched her burn. I scraped her up in my bare hands. She's no threat to you. She's nothing to you. She's gone. Things would be different if she were still here. I wouldn't be here, would I? You said you understood. I won't be bullied by you. I don't take orders from you. I'm sick of you telling me what to do. I'm not your *bitch*!"

She turns. Snaps. Starts making demands. Orders me out. Out of the room.

Tip her in the fucking sea. Go and don't come back. I'll tell him you're leaving. And if you stay against my wishes I'll tell him that too and he'll put you out on the street like the others. Dead like the others.

"Please don't make me do this", I say, my eyes shut tight.

How's your friend? Sam? The girl on the stairs. Mother fucking Theresa? She's cute. I like her. I hear she's been ill.

She laughs long and loud. It's all around me and I make myself small, crouched on the floor with my hands over my ears.

"Was it you?", I ask as the piercing laughter rattles the loose panes in their frames and jangles wire coat hangers in the wardrobe.

Oh, you're fighting for her. How sweet! Tell me Royal. Would you? I mean, if you could. If she asked you. Could you risk losing something that real?

"You are real. This is real", I say, standing stock still in the middle of the room.

To you, she says, *but not to anyone else. I need real too. A real man. Big and strong. Powerful. Someone who commands respect. Takes control. Not weak and weepy, scratching around in rubbish tips like a starving rat. Imaginary. You're imaginary, Royal. Made-up nonsense. You don't exist. You're nothing. Not like Clive.*

Clive, Clive, Clive. Clive this, Clive that. She wishes he was here. She wishes he'd knock on the door and take over. Pin her down. Take her against her will. Against the wall. All scratch and fight.

Shall I call him? Fucking limp-dick, soft-cock piece of shit, she howls. *Get Clive. A real man. Hung like a horse. Stiff as a stick. Clive knocked the cup over. I dared him. He ain't scared of you. He ain't scared of nuffink'. Because he's seen it all, mate. Fucking seen it all...*

I smash the radio on the floor and sweep the rest of the seashells off the windowsill, stamping on them, grinding them into the floor. Into dust. Then down the stairs and steps and out of the door, moving at speed towards the seafront and the beach and the wet slimy jetty revealed by the receding tide.

It's nearly dark and a wind rattles the halyards on the day boats and small cruisers a couple of hundred yards out. A tribal death song to accompany this final rite. And in the greyness of dusk I empty her ashes once and for all. What's left of sweet kind Lucy, burnt and abandoned and scattered between Hull and here. Pushed and pulled around like a toy. Just half a cupful, now gone.

And ripping the cup into little pieces, I toss them into the wind, blowing back at me in one final act of resistance, then dancing off up the beach. The rest sticking to the surface of the shallow water, bobbing with the wobble and jerk of the waves.

*

Sam looks out over the concrete and bricks and weeds and bins. The same drab vista. The same grey light.

She doesn't know if she has the energy to go back or go on. Everything seems so hopeless. Everything she says, every thought she has, frightens her. Each cigarette, harsh and dirty on her tongue.

"Let me know what you want to do", says Janet, killing the engine.

"I just need some time to think", says Sam. She wants to cry but doesn't. She wants to change her mind and tell Janet she'll come, but can't. It'd be a wasted trip. She'd burn that down too, she knows she would. Break it. Wreck it. Soil it. So what's the point?

"Just call me and I'll come and get you."

"I will."

"Promise me, Sam."

"I promise."

"No one's going to judge you. That's not how this works. I want you to be safe."

Janet's too involved. Sam needs to be on her own. She can feel it in her arms and legs. Twitching with frustration and irritation. She wants to lash out, resentment building to anger as she gets out of the car, not looking back. Clive appears at the top of the steps, his arms outstretched.

"Here she is!!", he sings.

She ignores him, blowing smoke up into the air, checking her phone.

"A letter came for you from the council. Do you want it?", he says brightly. Sam looks up. "Hold on, I've got it here". He rummages in his pocket, then holds up the flat of his hand and starts study it. "It says '*Dear Samantha Clark, you're never getting your kid back because you're a worthless piece of shit*'. That's what it says, right here. Right here in this letter."

Clive chuckles and wanders back inside the hotel. There's a confidence to him that she'd always struggled to fathom. He knew she'd be back. Never a doubt in his mind.

*

It's good news, the can money from the landfill. Regular money. Like a glue that can keep us together. Like a paste. Like an adhesive. Sticks us. So we're stuck. Stuck fast. Stuck here. That's good news, no? Yes. It's the best news. Because that's what we want, yes? It's regular money. To keep us together. That should be good news. Is it good news? Because I thought we both wanted the same thing. You don't have to do what I do. Not the work. The shit. The searching. The struggle. You just wait. Wait for me. You're always waiting. And watching. What's changed? Tell me what's changed? You do want me here don't you? This is what you want. Tell me. Jesus Christ. I can leave. Is that what you want? Do you want me to go? I was ready. Bang. Gone. Dead. But you stopped me because we fell in love, didn't we? You stopped me. Because we had something to live for. Both of us. I wanted to die, didn't I. Or is this some game? If it is, you must be having the time of your life. I won't go. Oh, no. You're stuck with me. Stuck like sticky paste. This ends when I say it does. I leave when I'm ready to leave. On my terms. You understand? Do you understand? Fucking answer me bitch. Tell me about Clive the Monster. You let him in here? Let him fuck you like a pig, because that's how he fucks people. Fucks them like pigs and treats them like dogs. Clive doesn't care about you. You're a fool. I gave up death for you. That was everything. A sacred death punctuating life. Puncturing it. Poisoned like Caesar. But you stopped me. Pulled me back then pulled me off. Acted coy like the little girl. You're no girl. Tell me what I can do to make you love me again. Please, I'm frightened. I still love you. I can forgive. Clive doesn't matter. Leave Clive to me. I'll sort Clive. Kill him if I have to.

*

I climb up to the top landing and Sam's door. It's unfamiliar territory. A strange land. The carpets, the layout, the colours, the smell. All the same. But the shadows are different and it's warmer. Part of a different routine. I hear footsteps behind the door. More a shifting of weight as the floorboards give and creak. Then she appears, tired and thin.

"I heard what happened", I say.

"Yeah?"

She goes back inside and I follow. It's smaller and darker than mine. Just the single window with boxes of her possessions stacked on one side, candlewax and fag ash all over the floor. I guess this is her home. It feels like a home. Something permanent. Not like mine. I was only supposed to stay one night. Not even that.

We stand in silence for a few seconds, processing the awkwardness and the intimacy of it. Me in her room. I've never been in a girl's room. Feels like a prelude to something. A changing of the guard. If it was the other way around there'd be consequences. The normal vitriol. Abuse and violence. Cruelty and bullying.

"What a fucking mess", she says and laughs, taking my hand, looking me in the eye. "Who do you argue with down there? I hear everything."

"I hear you too", I say.

"I'm trying to help you", she says.

"Then help yourself", I say.

"It's for my daughter."

"You could leave whenever you want."

"I have nowhere to go."

"It must be better than this."

She kisses me lightly on the cheek, letting it linger and spread to my lips. Her face is wet and cold. I feel her tongue at the corner of my mouth. Cigarettes and gum. Soft and sweet.

"We could go together", she whispers. "We can help each other."

"I can't."

"It doesn't make any sense."

"It does to me."

"We could look after one another."

"We don't have any money."

"What's wrong with me?", she asks, pushing me away.

"Nothing", I say, lying. It's not her, it's everything. Everything's wrong.

She opens the window and lights a cigarette, dabbing her wet cheeks with her cuff.

"I'll see you later then", she says abruptly and I leave.

Something has to change. Something has to give.

*

Ophelia lies in wait in the dark, sharpening her claws, curtains drawn. Scuffs of light, but mainly darkness and shadow. I can smell her. I can hear her breath.

Her voice is different. Gone is everything I knew. The soft lines and pastel colours. The curves and sweet perfume and giggles. She's tar-black and giant. Witch. Devil. Banshee. Monster. Ghost.

How was the kiss?

"What kiss?", I say, not looking up.

You kissed her. I saw you.

"*She* kissed *me*", I mutter, jaw clenched. I can't look at her.

D' you think I'm stupid? You think I don't see everything? I'm inside you. I see what you see. I'm there, laughing. Playing with you. You're right, it is a game. But you're not the first and you won't be the last. Go. You can scratch around in the dirt together. Rub your little soft cock against her. See how she likes it. I should have let you die. But why give you peace, when I can make you suffer? You think this is love, don't you? It's the opposite. Repulsion and disgust, man. All the time I was thinking about him. Him. How could I love you? I just wanted to see you work. Running around the streets looking for shit other people don't want. Don't need. Can't sell. You are that shit. Don't you see it?

It's too much. I was so close to death. So close to that peace. And she stopped me. Sent me off to fetch and carry and suffer and steal. The violence and sickness. The cold and wet. I see it now. It's all so clear.

I did this to myself. I let her in. Should have stuck to the path. To the plan. Things work when it's just me.

Looking around the room I plan my assault and escape.

I rip the curtain rail off the wall and attack her with it, gouging at the walls and the paper and plaster. Now it's her time to die.

She fights back, forcing me onto the floor. I roll under the bed, my hot burning cheeks jammed against the cold springs.
She's strong and everywhere, flipping the bed and ripping the headboard from the wall as the windows smash and curtains billow, sucked out by the salty wet wind. I push the wardrobe to escape her, scrambling clear. A huge crash that shakes the entire building.

She moves and darts like a demon. A horror film ghost. Old white-faced woman or eyeless child. Around the room, behind the debris, skipping across the ceiling like a giant black lizard. Suddenly the door flies open and Clive grabs me by my shoulders, pulling me towards the door, grabbing at my arms and legs. I bring my elbow down on the back of his head and spin back into the room. Ophelia, shrieking and cheering in my ear, counting me out. Her face is black melting plastic now. Zips for teeth. Arseholes for eyes.

Come on Clive! Do the cunt! she screams.

I lie on the floor with Clive on top of me, Ophelia's voice screaming at my insides. Clive is bleeding.

"Get the fuck out!", he shouts as the blood runs down his face like spilt paint. His arms suddenly around my waist. He has control.

"Please. I'll pay whatever you want. I'm sorry!"

"Get your shit and go", he says pushing me back inside. It's no use. There's no point. He's about to kill me. I've seen that look before. So I go. Not looking back, staggering down the passage and stairwell. Him behind me, breathing hard and jabbing me in the back while Ophelia floats above us. She's everywhere, watching and taunting.

Outside, a momentary sense of relief crushed by dread as the door is bolted behind me and he stalks back down the hall. I don't live there anymore.

Sam stands in silhouette at her window, and behind her Ophelia's red glowing eyes, her voice barely audible over the wind. Growling and cackling. The Omega People are dead. It's just me now.

Ophelia's gone rogue. Haunting the room unbeknown to the next poor fucker who breaks down outside. Lost and lonely. In need of peace or rest or death. Only to wander into one of her flesh-eating flowers and slowly dissolve.

Run away coward!, she sings over the rattling halyards. *Run away!*

She's following me. I can't run, so I beat away her mocking laughter with my own.

"Ha-ha-ha-ha-ha-ha-ha!"

I will defeat her. Fight fire with fire. No more tears. I'm stronger.

"Ha-ha-ha-ha-ha-ha-ha!"

I'll regenerate with the strength of her and a thousand like her. A new mantra now.

"YOU CAN'T HURT ME, YOU DON'T SCARE ME! YOU CAN'T HURT ME, YOU DON'T SCARE ME! YOU CAN'T HURT ME, YOU DON'T SCARE ME!"

The rattle of the trolley wheels adds weight as some boys in a Ford Fiesta hang out the windows, whooping and filming me on their phones. I spy her in the backseat, watching me. Sat amongst them. They can't see her but she talks straight into my head.

What about the child, she whispers.

"YOU CAN'T HURT ME YOU DON'T SCARE ME YOU CAN'T HURT ME YOU DON'T SCARE ME YOU CAN'T HURT ME YOU DON'T SCARE ME YOU CAN'T HURT ME YOU DON'T SCARE ME!"

But I'm having your child, she sings to silence me until all I can hear is the wind and all I can do is scream at the top of my lungs with my hands over my ears and my eyes on the ground. To keep her away, until I get to the landfill and play dead in the rubbish.

She can't hurt me there. The machines and the gulls and the rats will protect me.

"ARGHHHHHHHHHHHHHHHHHHHHHHHHHHHHHH!"

*

Clive unlocks Sam's door with his key and goes inside. She offers nothing, standing by the window watching Royal as he gathers his thoughts and things, pacing back and forth like a mad circus bear.

"Do you love him?"

"No"

"He doesn't love you."

"Where's Coco?", she asks.

"She's in the safe."

"Do you love me?"

"Forget about him."

She turns to face him. Smiling and strong. Teasing.

"That's why I'm here, isn't it? Because you love me and can't be without me. Do you want me, Clive? Come on. Coco's not here. No one will know." She takes him by the hand, pulling him towards her. "Come on, do it. I don't care anymore."

He says nothing, his cheeks wet with tears. She takes a step towards him and whispers in his ear. He trembles at her touch; at her voice. Then she kisses him and watches him leave, listening in silence to his lessening footsteps as he retreats to his basement.

IX.

The landfill is paradise. Giver of life. The concept of waste is absurd to me now. It's not waste, it's fruit and flesh. It's gold. It's treasure. It's life itself.

The machines are asleep. Recharging. Sucking down on seagull blood. Pulling them out of the sky far away from the seafront and its neon bullshit. I can smell the blood in the air. I know what they're doing. Planning their takeover. Hiding in plain sight. These aren't secrets any more. That bubble burst. I was desperate but I'm not desperate any more. I'm enlightened, and tired. I believe in everything. I've seen it all.

Who knows what happens next? I've stopped planning. Maybe I'll just sink into the earth, a fraction at a time. Slowly, gradually until I'm one with all this rubbish. Adding to it. Taking from it. Just part of the ecosystem. That'll show them. That'll shut them up. Scupper their little conspiracy.

I drag the trolley back to my trench, retrieve the neatly folded sheets and tarps I've collected over the past few weeks and start to build my home. Slowly at first, digging into the warm surface, hoping for a tunnel to heaven but settling for shelter from the wind and grit.

I'm alone for the first time in a long time, apart from the relentless plague of rats and gulls.

Ophelia can't hurt me here. This is my place now. My choice, for the first time in a lifetime. No fear. No dread. No dependence on another. Logan Bone or Ophelia. Or Clive. I'm dangerous because I don't care. I'll die here, looking out to sea, as the vermin pick and pull at my flesh and bones before they're crushed and ground into dust by the advancing machines and I simply cease to exist.

Maybe that's my goal. Not to find peace in life or peace in death. But just to not have existed at all. Human life is cheap, regardless of what they'll have you believe.

I'm one of the rats. One of the boys. Bigger and fatter and slower. Less experienced. Less savvy. Cleaner. With real hands and feet and opposable thumbs, but that means shit. It's wits and tenacity down here. The determination to survive at any cost. They will eat my thumbs.

I have seven pots for rainwater which I drain into old oil cans, boiling some for tea which I brew in empty soup tins. Bone broth from rotten chicken carcasses. I bind my new boots with salvaged string and electrical tape, and catch gulls with sticks and stones, breaking their necks and drinking their blood.

Bursting their little bitter pumping hearts into my mouth like grapes as gooey breast-feathers stick to my hands and chin. My face is black with dirt and the pungent grease of roasted rats, cooked on a homemade stove. Skewers, grills, knives and forks. Pots and pans. Setting traps to kill and maim, waking me up with their dying screams. Then smashing in their heads with rocks like I did Rag, before frying the mush into a savoury hash with garlic and onions and boiled potato peel. Beans if I'm lucky.

I scour the landfill for unfinished bottles and wineboxes, sucking whatever I can find out of the foiled plastic bags. Turning my face pink and making my head ache. Putting me to sleep and making me dream and believe I can fly and hover. No more waking at dawn, trudging up to Ray's. Taking beatings from gypsies and Ophelia.

And books. Hundreds of books. Big thick paperbacks. Novels and Magazines. Pornos. Fat white dimpled legs draped over old sofas or just lying on carpet as shapeless buttocks spread out beneath them like raw dough, pulling things back and shoving things in.

The Four Quartets. The New Testament, stained and swollen but readable. Danielle Steele.

I'm a sucker for love, but my heart will mend. And nothing will ever break it again.

Unless I fall for those beautiful machines on the smoky horizon. Me and my wandering eye. My fragile heart, like a seagull's. Easily caught. Easily crushed.

But when I'm alone in my tunnels? That's different. Dirty bastard, I am. Dirty stinking little terrier. Filthy pig. Who cares? Who's watching? It's up to me. It's my kingdom. Where I read about Jesus Christ and Bernie Fine and think and drink my wine and sleep and somehow drinking and thinking and sleeping and reading become the same thing and the books become wine and the wine becomes words.

I think about the hotel folk, searching for refuge and sanctuary and safety. And I'm no different to them. Traversing this God-awful country, running from past lives and uncertain futures. Floating in a weird suspension. Gas, fluid and solid. Every state possible. Alive and dead and everything in between. What are we fighting for? Some misplaced patriotism? What's Great Britain ever done for us?

Take Paintman. What was he protecting? A rubbish dump? Then what? Where did he go? Maybe he packed up and left. Maybe he saw that look in my eye and dug his own tunnel to the centre of the earth. Saw me doing all the things he wished he could, like hunting and killing and boozing and cooking and magicking water out of the sky, and thought better of it.

Maybe he saw me bury the battle-scarred and charred bodies of the Omega People and dug on down with his thick gloved hands until he found a new world of his own.

Or maybe he died, flattened and compacted by the beautiful machines that call to me across the rubbish flats, looking for attention like those young Spanish boys whistling at girls in their confirmation dresses.

*

On the eighth day I talk to God and he presents me gifts. A plastic carrier bag inside a shoebox in another bag, taped up tight and tied with string like a Christmas present. Inside is my future. The future of everyone. What I'd been waiting for. Why I was digging. It wasn't a tunnel to the centre of the earth, but a quest to find the bag in a box in another bag bound with tape and string. And inside that, a bundle of money and an antique pistol.

The proceeds of a bungled crime. A murder weapon perhaps. The money dumped with it, in error. Hidden for later and thrown out by an unsuspecting relative or in a fit of conscience. But probably just lost in the chaotic aftermath of some drug deal gone wrong and hidden in fear.

It's an instruction. An invitation. Can't be anything else. Money and death. I've hunted high and low for both and here it is in equal measure.

If I'd had the gun when I arrived it would have been over. If I'd had the money, I'd still be there. It could be a choice, but I see it as an instruction. The natural order of things.

They've been keeping me in the dark, revealing the plot gradually and my role in it. But this is it now. Finally. This is what they were saving me for.

I was lost. Digging my tunnel. Becoming rubbish heap. The weeks spent officiating at the funerals of the Omega People, millions of them. Committing them to the ground. Scattering petals and words from scripture. The sun, the moon, the sea and the earth. Fire and water. Love and Kindness. I'd created from this mountain of rubbish something the earth and the heavens hadn't managed in their complete history. Something God himself couldn't even manage.

Because the world they created failed and the people turned on each other, poisoned by hallucinogenics and drink, and chemicals in the food. But no one gets it right first time. Practice makes perfect. Learn by your mistakes. Pass the baton.

If at first you don't succeed look to the landfill. That's why they sent for me. That's why they killed Lucy and sent me away, over the hills to Ophelia and the sea, to confront my pain. Every catastrophic failure contributing to this one final triumph.

Rising into the sky in a ball of white fire to a paradise of my own creation.

And the gun and the money are a sign. A message.

Time's up. I'm a soldier of God. I am God. The God of Rubbish. My kingdom of filth. Created in a week. And with this gift the transformation is complete. Like a regeneration or metamorphosis. The creator of the new world. This dump will support all life, created and overseen by me.

I sit in my narrow lair loading and unloading the gun. Counting the bullets. Squeezing the trigger, sat on a crate embedded in the surface. Sinking with my weight.

She can't have the child. Not without me. Not the fruit of a trick. She cannot mother the son of God. A whore like Mary Magdalene? A charlatan and heretic. I will die for their sins. For their suffering. Die to set them free. And the child will die with me.

Me. The next God. The new God. The latest God. Lured away to Hotel Ophelia by the devil himself. It's clear now. So clear.

Clive is the Devil, and he saw to it that I deviate from that one true path, physically wrestling the poison from my lips and shining orange light straight into my stupid thirsty heart and eyes. Blinding me and sending me tumbling off course. Then giving Ophelia my seed before casting me out like a leper. Reduced to a beggar on the freezing streets, to a wretch on these rubbish piles.

*

It's warmer now and the flies swarm and buzz around my camp. Attracted by the animal remains and shit and gulls' heads hanging off the line. But they don't bother me. They're part of the transformation. Transformative themselves, as they lay their eggs in the bird heads which wriggle with maggots and new life.

Some of the gulls are machines though. Government drones sent to spy. The eyes in the sky. Swooping down, feigning desperation and hunger for a closer look. I know your game. Nothing gets past me.

*

Paintman's back.

His rocks raining down on me with familiar cracks and bangs. Hitting my pots and cans. I reach for protection. The helmet I saved for exactly this. A gouge at the top and flat spot from a high-speed crash. The black veneer cracked and flaking.
Maybe whoever owned the helmet owned the gun and stole the money. A high-speed chase through narrow streets and housing estates, egged on by their own in a blur of blue lights.

I've been waiting for you, Paintman. Coward.

He was hiding all this time. But I'm not scared of Paintman. You or anything else. It's my reward for suffering and martyrdom. The new religion. The new church. Worship this, *muthafucker.*

I walk across the hollow in my helmet, taped boots, and improvised waterproofs. Down into the valley and up the other side as the rocks bounce off me. I feel nothing. No pain. I'm in his image. We are one and the same. I've played him at his own game and won.

He tracks me, watching as I climb up the bank, tripping and faltering, his arms at his sides, powerless against God. Ready to serve. In my image. Just a few inches apart now, visor to visor.

"Take off your helmet", I say.

He doesn't. His human eyes blinking through the cracked plastic.

"Take off your helmet", I repeat, pointing the gun at his chest.

He does what he's told this time and I see myself as a younger man. The child at the start of the journey. Fresh-faced and frightened, of sex and God and being alone, with sunken cheekbones and slender frame beneath all those layers of patchwork rags and plastic bags.

I raise the pistol to his chest and shoot out his heart as hundreds of gulls take to the skies and he falls to the ground. Paintman's dead. Murdered and martyred. He died for us. For me.

He died so I could live and set them free, saving him from himself.

I drag him down into the tunnel and I cover his face and canonise him and spend the night with his body at the entrance to our tomb, dug deep into the landfill looking out over the Estuary. And I sit and cry tears of joy because I'm free. No longer running. Free to kill devils and emancipate mankind. Because we've all been lied to for far too long.

It's time to leave. I can't stay here. This was Paintman's all along. The gentle ecosystem – him and the machines – living side by side for thousands of years. Then I arrived and changed everything. Drove him away. Objectified the machines and sent him away to regroup, before murdering him – me – and burying him in a hole. But that's what change is.

Nothing stays the same. It can't.

*

I wait till dark, avoiding the glare of seafront, cutting up instead towards the petrol station by the huge empty carpark. The petrol's greasy on my hands as I fill the containers, burning and stinging my torn finger nails and cuticles. All the nicks and cuts and scratches. There's a light floaty rain swarming in the streetlamps like flies or snow.

The attendant watches me leave without paying. Watches me watching him behind his counter and reinforced glass. Safe amongst the fags and chocolate and pasties. He's not safe out here. He knows that.

Me, black as tar and oil, casually strolling away without care or conscience. I don't know what I look like. What day it is. Wild-eyed and unrecognisable as the rain runs down my face and through my beard. It tastes of sweat and smoke and iron. Strength.

Anything can happen out here. I'm king. I'm dangerous. I don't care anymore. And when you don't care nothing can touch you. When you no longer fear consequence there's no punishment left. So what if I die? That was the plan all along. Right from the start. I will die. I'm about to die. I've decided.

It'll be on the news. Screen-grabbed and blown up. Loner. Escapee. Messiah. God.

All the questions. How was it allowed to happen? Why was it not picked up? How do people just disappear? Walk out of secure facilities never to be seen again. Was anyone looking for him? Who was looking after him? They'll look at the faxes and the emails between the hospital and the health authority. The whole thing will unravel like a bobbin. No hiding places. Then Clive. Who was he? Where did he come from? How was he able to do what he did for so long right under everyone's noses?

The system will be overhauled. Every rock and rotten tree trunk lifted to reveal the teeming creatures underneath, in the dark and wet, as they zig-zag away. The building demolished and sold off, kickstarting the redevelopment of the street, the area, the town. Part of my legacy. They'll fucking thank me. Discuss it in the Commons.

They'll bring in the Ophelia Bill, protecting immigrants and the vulnerable from devils like Clive who suck their souls right out of their bodies and fuck their children as distant families wonder where they are. And the spirit of the Omega People will live on.

Hotel of Horrors. That's what they'll call it in the papers as their people ask questions and file stories from local hotels. *Kept himself to himself. Stopped by from time to time with trinkets to sell or looking for work. Seemed like a nice man. Gentle. Didn't say much. But come to think of it, there was something strange about him.*

Who knows. Who cares. But I need to act. I need to save those people. Their children. Their lives.

Dear old Logan. He wasn't the villain afterall. Not compared to this. Just some drunk old queen with the bit between his teeth. The three of us living quite comfortably in that house until he burned it all down. Fool. We could have been happy. Could have made it work.

Maybe if I hadn't hidden the bottle. Maybe if I'd just stepped over him on my way to the CD player like I'd done so many times before. Maybe if I'd apologised and told him it wouldn't happen again. Shown him some respect instead of lashing out.

Doobie was right. There are unicorns. There is magic. This is just the shit bit. You have to dig deeper. There'll be something after this. Maybe not paradise but something. It can't just be this, surely.

*

The hotel's dark and I feel invisible. The only sound, fuel sloshing and butting against the inside of the containers as I walk, and the squeak of my hard taped boots. I stand a while watching from the darkness, imagining a different life. The Ophelia I fell in love with. Shy and nubile. Sweet-smelling and smooth. Not the oozing fanged shapeshifter that emerged.

Hag and whore.

I push the door and go slowly up the stairs, conscious of every step and creak. It smells the same but I smell different. The filth of faith. The reek of God. Along the familiar landing where I'd creep back with my shells and pennies. Star-crossed. Weak with love and dreams and hunger.

But not now. I'm hard now. Fortified by fox flesh and gull hearts and wine. Greased and oiled. Ready for the fight and flight.

A small wiry bare-chested smackhead opens the door to room 21, peering up blearily through his opiate dream, skin the colour of moonrock.

"Who the fuck are you?", he says.

"I'm the saviour of mankind", I say.

"Get fucked", he says stepping back as if to close the door.

I jam my large taped boot in the frame and point the gun at his forehead, speaking very slowly so he can't help but understand the danger he's in. I don't have time for a fight or situation. I will kill anyone who gets in my way. Devils or otherwise.

"If you stay, you die", I say.

I'm giving him a chance. A choice. A way out. Not so cocky now. He thinks. He processes. Slowly. His basic brain overloaded by smack and gin. He's paid for the room and the gear. Wanted to make a night of it. Left alone with his addiction. Just the two of them.

"Is it about Monkey's mum's broach?", he stutters.

At last he's seen the danger. His eyes are full of self-pity. Creating a lie. It comes so easy. Like breathing air.

"No it's nothing to do with Monkey's mum's broach", I say. "It's about the fate of mankind", and I push him back into the room - my room, my love - and hold the gun to his head while he stuffs his meagre possessions into a vinyl sports bag. Phone and charger. A bobbly fleece. His gear and fags and lighter in a small tin box. Stumbling out, broadsiding the door-frame in his unsteady desperation to get away.

It's not mine anymore. It's different. It smells different. Smells of him. His odour. Drug smoke. No heart on the wall now. That's gone. No softness or love. 'Clive!", I scream. "Clive!", and I sit on the bed in the darkness and wait.

Ophelia emerges from the dark recess. In a change of temperature. She's frightened. Shocked by my appearance. Terrified of what I've become and what I'm capable of, sensing my power and intention. She asks me why I've come back. Says she's pleased to see me. Says she's missed me and still loves me. She's lying, scared for the baby and Clive.

"Where is he?", I ask calmly.

Who? she asks.

Who? As if you don't know. Don't pretend. I'm not stupid.

"Clive the Devil", I say. I don't mention the child. I can't. She'll run and warn Clive. And they'll escape. I can't afford for that to happen. So I keep her calm, the fuel at my feet, edging it into the valance so she can't see it.

How should I know? she says. *I don't care about Clive. I only care about you. That's why I'm so pleased you're back. Pleased you're here. Back where you belong. Where we belong. A family. A proper family, like you always wanted. Like you never had. This child will be loved. Not ignored and abandoned. Truly loved.*

"Don't talk to me about love", I say. "You don't know what love is."

I do. I love you. We can fix this. We can be together. Just you and me. Here. It doesn't have to be like this. Please Royal!

"I'm sick of your fucking lies. Just get Clive. I want to talk to him. Got something for him. Gonna show him who I am. Go and get him."

But he's already on his way. Floating p the stairwells and along the corridors. A shadow beneath the door. He could appear in a puff of smoke but doesn't know I know, so assumes human form. Maintaining his little charade.

The door swings open and he stands there in stockings and suspenders and glittery see-through plastic stripper heels, his face painted red and white like a Victorian doll's, a hairnet across his bare scalp held fast by elastic. Wigless.

His cock and balls bunched and flattened by the pink silk panties. A tight pink bra cutting across his nipples and grey chest hair.

“What are you doing here?”, he growls, taking it all in. My bloodshot eyes sunk deep in my blackened face. Rat fat and gull blood. Booze. Piss and shit. She’s frightened. Something I haven’t seen before. I don’t question her appearance. I don’t care. I know what’s underneath.

“I know all about it”, I say.

“All about what?”, he asks.

“Why you brought me here. Who you’re working for.”

He laughs. “What the fuck are you talking about!?”

“You know exactly what I’m talking about.”

I’m not here to talk. I’m not looking for answers. He takes a step towards me and I shoot him. Once in the chest and once in the groin. He falls to the ground and crawls towards the corner of the room. All arms and legs. Castrated and cockless at long last. What’s left of it hanging between his legs like flappy bloodied entrails.

He knows it’s the end. It’s a beautiful moment of stillness and mutual understanding. Respect even. A new dynamic as his lungs fill with blood and he starts to drown. Gurgling wildly. Some vain protestation probably, but far too late. Never bring stilettos to a gun fight. Never.

I take his keys and lock the door. I must die so others can live. I must die for his sins. It says so in scripture. I must deliver them from evil. Set them free. Prize open the gates of hell and let these poor fuckers out.

*

An alarm sounds. It's deafening. Mechanical. Metal on metal. I can feel it in my knees and my teeth, groan above and below me. Frightened voices behind the twelve double-locked doors. Sam appears on the landing. She doesn’t recognise me.

"Sam!"

She turns and looks at a stranger. Part man, part beast, part rubbish dump.

"Royal? Where have you been?"

I give her the bag of money.

"What's this?", she asks.

"It's for you. You need to leave. Get as far away from here as possible."

"What about you?"

"Don't worry about me", I say as the landing and stairs fill up with people and children, everyone carrying something. A box or a bag.

"I'll come and find you. Please go. It's not safe."

She drifts towards the stairwell, turning back just once before disappearing with the others.

Back in room 21 Clive's still alive, sapped of energy and fight, his stilettos turned out on the floor. This wasn't how it was supposed to end. But this is how it will end.

Blood soaks his underwear and kimono a dark shiny red, his face glowing green as he bleeds out. I uncap the petrol and splash it over his head and chest. He winces and groans as the fuel fills his wounds, but he's half dead and his fight has gone.
Ophelia kneels at his side, doing her best to stem the bleeding. Pathetic. Her dying warrior. Tears in her eyes.

"I told you it was for life. And life means life. You did this to yourself", I bark at her.

“What... the... fuck... are... you... talking... about... you... mad... cunt?”, gasps Clive in a defeated whimper, a short dying breath between each word.

I hold up the cigarette lighter - thumb poised - and he starts to scream. Finding something from somewhere. Terror and acceptance.

“Please... I’m... sorry. I... don’t... know... what this... is. Have... what ... you... want. I’ll ... pay... you...”

"SHUT UP!", I scream. "SHUT THE FUCK UP! IT’S TOO LATE FOR DEALS! I KNOW WHO YOU ARE! I’VE SEEN WHAT YOU DO!”

Ophelia interrupts. Tells me I’m wrong. It’s not what I think. He’s a good man. A kind man. He deserves a second chance. I’ve got it all wrong. Clive’s on our side.

I tell her to be quiet. I’ve heard enough. Had enough. The game's up. Staring back at her. Into her. At the wall, with my X-Ray vision. Her black lungs and heart. The foetus in her womb, squirming like a slug as Clive summons his remaining strength to crawl towards the door. One final desperate lunge for freedom. I kick him with my taped boots, stamping on his head and hands, breaking his fingers as he curls into a ball.

Then I douse myself in the rest of the petrol. Soaking my head and hair. Running down the inside of my homemade suit and legs. The bleach, a lifetime ago.

Fuel now. In my eyes, my mouth, my ears. Stinging the back of my throat. My black hands are smooth and greasy. I can see Logan and Bernie and Afzal on a fairground carousel, waving at Lucy. Clive starts to moan. Another weak bloodless protest, through the wobble of fumes.

“You’re free, Clive. We all are”, I say as I squeeze the lighter with my thumb, flicking the striker wheel against the stubborn flint.

She never really got to the bottom of it. The voices and shouting and shells and shit. But whatever it was, whatever it all meant, it mattered to him as he tried and failed to find answers.

Royal was a kind man. A good man. But Clive was special. He had something. Something she couldn't quite fathom. He'd survived this long for a reason. A real fucking human. Evil. Strong. Sick. Hard. Perfectly evolved for this world like a cockroach.

Maybe she did love him after all. But it didn't matter now. All that chaos and confusion simply returned to the earth like nothing happened.

*

Bullish cops usher the bewildered crowd up the street and away from danger as the fire crews vainly attempt to contain the rapidly expanding inferno.

Where will they sleep tonight? Where will they sleep tomorrow? Maybe the church will take them in. Put mats down and give them tea and biscuits. Drum up some community support. Even if they are foreign.

Sam hurries off up the street virtually unnoticed as the fire rages behind her, gobbling up the germs and dirt, disinfecting everything it touches. Her bed and books and trauma. One hand on the money in her coat pocket. She can feel the heat on her neck as shadows lengthen and merge. The briefest memory of bonfire night as a child.

There are tears in her eyes. Tears for Royal and Clive. Tears for Janet and Jody. Tears for the world. Tears for everyone in it. Tears for the future. Tears for the fucking wretched state of everything.

While she's observed closely from above by a robot gull *JCB/EVB-18072206* beaming live images back to control. And a mile away on the East Beach a unicorn nuzzles the washed up remains of a rotting mermaid, licking her hair and face. Her ribs exposed and a stomach full of silt and micro-plastics.

Toxicology will reveal heroin, crystal meth, nicotine and a blood alcohol level of 187mg.

And in that moment a black van arrives in the dunes and the government men appear to retrieve the body, as the unicorn retreats up the beach unseen, gouging the wet sand with pure white hoofs as the surf rushes in to cover its tracks.

The End.

Follow Hotel Ophelia on Instagram
at hotelophelia_novel

Printed in Great Britain
by Amazon

33477555R00118